Shell Game

CHRIS KENISTON

Indie House Publishing

MORE BOOKS
By Chris Keniston

Hart Land
Heather
Lily
Violet
Iris
Hyacinth
Rose
Calytrix
Zinnia
Poppy
Picture Perfect

Farraday Country
Adam
Brooks
Connor
Declan
Ethan
Finn
Grace
Hannah
Ian
Jamison
Keeping Eileen
Loving Chloe
Morgan
Neil

Honeymoon Series
Honeymoon for One
Honeymoon for Three
Honeymoon for Four
Honeymoon for Five

Aloha Romance Series:
Aloha Texas
Almost Paradise
Mai Tai Marriage
Dive Into You
Look of Love
Love by Design
Love Walks In
Shell Game
Flirting with Paradise

Surf's Up Flirts:
(Aloha Series Companions)
Shall We Dance
Love on Tap
Head Over Heels
Perfect Match
Just One Kiss
It Had to Be You
Cat's Meow

ACKNOWLEDGEMENTS

There are not enough words to thank Dale Rogers for giving up valuable vacation time and sharing countless stories of his early Navy days as well as patiently explaining the workings of a submarine. I have oodles of inspiring notes and hope to do them justice on these pages and future books.

For showing me the proper way to use a treadmill for a five mile run in the sand, letting me snap photo after photo so I wouldn't forget and patiently helping me learn Aussie speak, Ships Personal Trainer Tyler Dickson.

I owe a special thank you to my friends Jim and Diane Borgia for taking me on relaxing rides along the Long Island shore, letting me linger in the calm breezes of their backyard for as long as I wanted, and keeping me honest with daily word count. You guys define long lasting friendship. And to David Pohle not only do I say thank you for your willing helpful input, but write that book!

Any mistakes are all mine and no reflection on these wonderful people!

Enjoy and Mahalo!

PROLOGUE

Somewhere near the Afghan border

Whiskey *Tango Foxtrot—WTF*. From his rooftop perch Luke "Brooklyn" Chapman had a clear shot at the last barrier between his team and the American journalist they'd been assigned to bring home. Only two things stood in his way. Enough C4 to blow not only the entire compound but also every member of his SEAL team and Nick Harper's Explosive Ordnance Disposal team to kingdom come—and the woman wearing the frigging explosives.

Do not pass Go. Do not collect two hundred dollars. *Blast…*

Intel had screwed with them again. Brooklyn had gotten wind on his own of possible mines and other booby traps along the target compound that official channels had discarded as unreliable. That was why Brooklyn was once again working with EOD. He'd requested Nick's team for this mission, and, royally ticked off with the increased stream of failed missions, his CO had approved it. Nick and his team were good. Very good. The best. And Brooklyn trusted them as much as his own men. Which was something rare for a frogger to admit.

"Team Bravo reporting, target spotted. We have confirmation on explosives. C4. Over."

"Can you take him out? Over."

"Her," Brooklyn corrected.

Nick mumbled an obscenity on the other side.

Tell me about it. Protecting women and children was etched in bold caps on the unwritten list of what military men were fighting for—right above Mom's apple pie and just under the American Way. Over time Brooklyn had grown used to dealing with hostiles of varied ages and sizes—but he'd never get used to fighting women. And the key question at hand was whether or not this particular female was in harm's way of her own free will or by order of some male family member.

Too often there was not enough time to determine if the explosive-wearing fashionistas were the former or the latter. In this case, Brent Callahan, one of the EOD team, was on the surveillance systems. Thanks to his Persian heritage on his mother's side and having spent over a year at the Defense Language Institute, Brent could eavesdrop in five languages spoken within a one-mile radius. If the female in question would only say something in the next few seconds allotted to determine friendly or enemy, Brooklyn's last kill for Uncle Sam's Navy might not have to be a woman.

Across the way on Team Alpha, Billy "King Kona" Everrett and Doug Hamilton, rappelled down the south wall. Kenny Yates and Nick, Team Charlie, were nowhere to be seen. Which meant the hostiles couldn't see them either. The difference being Brooklyn knew his buddies were positioned to have Team Alpha's six.

Brother, how he wished Brent would speak up. In about fifteen seconds Billy would be in place, and Brooklyn would have to take the woman out. *Ten…. Five.*

"Hold your fire," Brent said in Brooklyn's earpiece. "Make that two hostages."

Whoever the woman was, Brent must have heard enough to know wearing this season's dynamite trend was not her idea. Brooklyn spoke into his mic. "Affirmative."

"Copy," Nick replied, followed by Billy's echo of the confirmation.

This unlucky woman would live to see another day. All the team had to do was diffuse the jacket, subdue the enemy and haul everyone's six out of hell.

"Nice place you got here." Brooklyn filed in last and dropped his gear beside the other duffels on the living room floor of EOD team member Billy Everrett's Kona, Hawaii, home. After getting everyone's butt out of the Afghan compound and safely returning to base with both hostages—the American journalist and the now bomb-free woman—Brooklyn was more than glad the timing had worked out for him to join some of the guys on leave here on the Big Island. A last chance to be among his navy brothers that he didn't want to miss.

"The house is still a work in progress, but it's home." Billy pointed down the hall. "You've got four bedrooms to flip for. Mom always comes by to clean up the place for me when I'm back in Kona on leave. She texted that she changed the sheets for you guys, and I'm guessing there'll be a fridge full of food."

Nick, the EOD team leader, grabbed his bag to claim his room. Two steps behind him, Brent Callahan, a SEAL team mate, flashed his pearly whites. "And beer?"

"I said *my mother*." Billy rolled his eyes. "This isn't Australia. No locals leaving beer for sailors on this pier."

Kenny Yates, another of Brooklyn's SEAL team members, hefted his duffel and headed down the hallway. "How about women?"

Two steps behind him Brooklyn reached forward and slapped Kenny on the back. "Doubt his mom put those in the fridge either."

"Comedian." Kenny, originally from the Northeast, hip-checked Brooklyn as he walked by. In a blink, duffels were dropped, and the two men were on the ground.

"I swear, Brooklyn." Making his way across the room and down the hall in a heartbeat, Billy towered over the two tussling men. "One dent in my new walls and I'll have both your sixes on a platter."

"Sorry, man," Kenny mumbled, catching Brooklyn's eye as he pushed to his feet. Having been on the same SEAL team for the last few years, words weren't required for communication. A turn, a lunge and a tackle later, all three were on the ground.

Brent emerged from the front bedroom and nearly got pulled into the fray. "I can think of better ways to work up a sweat, guys."

"He's right." Kenny eased back, and Billy took advantage of the shift in leverage to dump both SEALs on their sixes.

"Never mess with King Kona." Brushing his hands together, Billy spun about. "Clean up, and we'll hit the strip. It's no Gauntlet, but even you ugly frogs should be able to find a girl to take pity on you."

Showered, shaved and once again looking like a clean-cut sailor instead of a rebel insurgent, Brooklyn and his buddies walked into one of Billy's favorite local haunts. A splattering of pretty tourists decorated the place. Not near as many options as Honolulu and nothing at all like walking the famed foreign street known to sailors worldwide as The Gauntlet. But then again, few places were.

Brooklyn's introduction to The Gauntlet hadn't been long after earning his Trident and graduating from Coronado. The memory was still vivid. His team had gone in country on a reconnaissance mission and caught a ride offshore back to base on a Fast-Attack submarine. A fortuitous choice for transportation. En route, the sub had port call, and Brooklyn was introduced to The Gauntlet's hairpin strip of clubs and bars.

There, women of all shapes and sizes spilled onto the streets vying for their shot at an American sailor. Every few yards one of his group would be yanked aside and disappear into the open bars. A few would survive the barrage of women pawing and kissing to make it to the next one, usually sans a shirt, belt or some other article of clothing, and always bathed in lipstick and perfume.

Down to only a handful of men still walking, Brooklyn spotted a tall, lanky gal with long auburn hair. "I think I might be in the mood for a redhead."

One of the senior team members glanced over his shoulder and smiled. "Well, you'd better keep walking because *that guy* is probably a brunette."

"Hey." Brent waved his hand in front of Brooklyn's

face snapping him back to the present. "Where did you go?"

Holding back a grin, he shrugged a shoulder. "Window-shopping."

All four friends cut him a curious glance before turning their attention back to a particularly interesting table of young ladies old enough to legally drink and young enough to make these sailor's night.

Across the room a few guys walked in the front door. One wore a Don't Tread on Me T-shirt, another sported an American flag tattoo and all had the regulation haircuts that screamed US Navy. Probably stationed at Pearl. And like Brooklyn and his buddies, creatures of habit. Give a sailor a day off, and he goes looking for beer and girls. Not a bad way to live.

"You're starting to worry me, Brooklyn." Billy pointed the neck of his beer bottle at him. "Wipe that crazy grin off your face."

"Aye, Chief." Brooklyn gave a weak salute. His last one. From now on he belonged to The Company. Six months ago he'd seen a mighty fine squadron of SEALs give up their lives due to bad intel. Intel provided by the CIA and their network of informants. So Brooklyn had requested separation from the US Navy and aligned himself with the very people who had gotten too many good men killed with planted information.

Next time Kenny, Brent and the rest of Brooklyn's former team members got intel through the CIA, Brooklyn would do his damnedest to make sure the info wouldn't get anyone killed. Or he'd die trying.

CHAPTER ONE

Two years later

The black-and-white from Miami PD pulled into Sharla Kramer's driveway.

Not again.

Tyler Hawk, former partner of her late husband, Danny, eased out of the driver seat. His expression blank, he opened the back door and out popped Sophia Garibaldi.

Not that Sharla had expected to see anyone else. At all of five foot two and a hundred pounds soaking wet, her grandmother still managed to cause more trouble than a rabbit in a lettuce patch. "Nana. Not again."

"Don't fuss. Tyler offered me a ride."

Sharla's gaze met Tyler's. Lips pressed tightly together, the six-foot-four policeman ran his hand across the back of his neck before speaking. "We picked her up at the mall."

"Nana," Sharla whined. "You promised."

"I didn't do anything." The older woman straightened her proud shoulders and lifted her stubborn chin. "That daft head of security called the police over a little misunderstanding."

Ever since Nana had retired to Florida to live with Sharla, "a little misunderstanding" had become the three most unsettling words in the English language.

"A shopper at the discount shoe store insisted your grandmother tried to pick her pocket. Said she saw Sophia's hand coming out of her purse just as the woman was about to pay for her purchases."

Sharla turned to her grandmother. "You had her wallet?"

"No," Tyler answered. "But the woman insisted she'd

merely foiled your grandmother's attempt to steal it."

"Poppycock." Nana huffed. "If I'd wanted—"

"Yes, Nana, we know." Sharla cut off her grandmother before she could incriminate herself. Not that Tyler wasn't fully aware of the family history. He'd already been partnered with Danny when he had started dating Sharla and had witnessed firsthand the antics of her crazy family as they, one by one, retired—supposedly—to Florida. It was almost enough to make her want to move to Alaska. Or anyplace no one would be tempted to follow her.

Tyler waited until Sophia had crossed the doorway into the kitchen. "We've got lots of new rookies on board since… well, new guys who didn't know Danny."

Sharla bobbed her head. Tyler didn't have to say anything else. "I understand. Thanks for bringing her home. I'll go to the mall tomorrow after my shift at the hospital and have another talk with Mr. Delvecchio."

"You okay otherwise?"

Tyler flashed his trademark killer smile that would make most women weak in the knees. Especially if they were gazing into his crystal-blue eyes. A light, almost-gray shade of blue, they always twinkled with a little mischief no matter how serious the situation. But it had been Danny's reserved smile and warm chocolate eyes that had stolen her heart the first time he'd arrived at her apartment door with her great-aunts Alicia and Leticia in tow. "I'm fine. Thanks."

After Danny's funeral, Tyler had kept frequent tabs on her. At first she was glad for the company. Someone to talk to who knew Danny almost as well as she did. As the months passed by, she realized she couldn't keep living her life with Danny through shared memories. Eventually Tyler's calls and visits came less often. And now, three years later, she mostly only saw Tyler when he'd swoop in to rescue one of the great-aunts or, like tonight, her grandmother.

"You'll let me know if—"

"I need anything," Sharla finished for him with a smile. "Thanks again, Ty."

Front door latched shut, Sharla spun about and leaned back. What was she going to do with her nimble-fingered relatives? At least starting in a few days the next month would be surprise-free. While Great-Aunt Alicia visited her daughter in California for the summer, Nana and Great-Aunt Leticia were going on another Caribbean cruise and then planned to visit old friends in New York for a couple of weeks. As long as Nana and her former cohorts had an audience to entertain with their old stories, Sharla could rest assured they would stay out of trouble.

She hadn't heard the phone ring, but Nana's voice carried from the kitchen, "Oh my. Really?"

Upon closer observation, Sharla was not happy with the look on her grandmother's face.

"No, Ticia. Maybe I should—"

Sharla walked closer and leaned into her grandmother's side in an effort to eavesdrop on the phone conversation, but Nana wished her sister well and hung up. "What's the matter? Is there a problem with Nelda?"

"Not exactly. The baby decided to turn at the last minute. Doctors did a C-section. Ticia wants to stay and help while Nelda recovers."

The news wasn't as bad as Sharla had feared. Until it hit her why her grandmother's forehead was crinkled with concern. The cruise left on Thursday. No way Nelda would be a 100 percent by then for Leticia to go as planned.

In a snap Nana's expression cleared, a bright smile taking over her face. "Didn't your boss just say you had too many vacation days accumulated and you needed to take time off while he had the staff to cover for you?"

Actually, yes. She'd already penciled in two weeks while Nana was away. The perfect time to get in a little sun and tinker with some long-neglected household proj... "Oh, no."

"Of course. The cruise company said we could add passengers up to twenty-four hours before departure. You can have Leticia's place. Like the old days when your parents would be off on some adventure and the two of us would spend time on the Jersey shore."

"No, Nana." *Absolutely not. No how. No way.* Sharla was not spending two weeks trapped on a floating hotel in the middle of the ocean. "So not happening, Nana. There is nothing you can say to get me on that boat with you."

"Maybe Magda would like to join me."

Except that. The last thing Sharla needed was for her grandmother to reconnect with her old partner in crime. Heaven help her, it looked like she and Nana were going on a cruise.

Ignoring the burn still present in his side, Luke "Brooklyn" Chapman tried to relax into the stiff guest chair and propped his ankle across his thigh. The thick leather belt he'd worn that day when all hell had broken loose had slowed the knife enough to prevent any serious damage, especially since the stupid thing had been dipped in poison. Two years of deep undercover work had finally paid off. A little field needlework, some antidotal treatment and he was good to go.

Too bad the doc hadn't agreed.

"Thirty days. That's an order."

Disregarding the tug from the medic's stitches, Brooklyn shifted in place and flashed a cocky grin at his supervisor. "You can't give me an order. I'm not in the navy anymore."

"You won't be with *anybody* anymore if you don't take some downtime. I don't care how invincible you SEALs think you are. You are made of flesh and blood like everyone else. You cut. You bleed. You die. I don't want to see your face or hear your name for thirty days."

In the navy, as SEALs on standby, Brooklyn and his men were limited to two beers a day and an hour-long leash, never allowed to be more than sixty minutes away from base. A few days of true R & R when they would be free to indulge in all the booze and women they could handle was always embraced with much anticipation. But usually after only a few days of rest and recreation, he'd been ready to go back to work. And not just busy work or physical training. Something worthy of his time and all that constant PT. "I'll take a couple of days."

"Thirty."

"But—"

"Listen, Brooklyn." Phil Conway leaned forward on his desk. "I know you want to see all these bastards fry as much as any of us."

More. Under the umbrella of the CIA, in a joint task force with the navy commanded by Admiral Cartwright, Brooklyn, along with a former ranger and another spook, had infiltrated the terrorist cell believed to have been behind the faulty intel that had gotten a squadron of SEALs killed almost three years ago.

The recent firefight that had left Brooklyn with a knife in his gut had also taken out the SOBs responsible for the death of his fellow SEALs. But there was always another terrorist waiting to step up and annihilate "the American infidels." When the terrorists took R & R, then so would he.

"You are running on caffeine and adrenaline," Conway continued. "Something's got to give sooner or later, and it's not going to be on my watch."

For a spook Conway was a decent guy, but he didn't get it. Brooklyn could remind his boss from now till the next millennium what every SEAL endured for months of basic training. Constant harassing by professional warriors with one objective: eliminate the weak. Only the strongest and smartest survived Hell Week and BUD/S. Long torturous runs in the soft sand. Midnight swims in the cold Pacific. Arduous obstacle courses. Never-ending calisthenics. Days without sleep. Always being cold, wet and miserable.

And the training didn't stop there. The training never stopped. In the real world, lack of sleep and physical endurance was a way of life. SEALs thrived on stress and chaos. He didn't need thirty days with nothing to do.

"Got anyplace you've always wanted to go?" Conway asked. "Family you haven't seen for a while?"

Some downtime home in New York with the family

would be good. Even with his mother hovering over him, it would be great to see his sisters and nieces and nephews. And it had been a while since he'd had a decent lasagna. But thirty days?

He could always throw a dart at a map and see where it landed. There were plenty of possible destinations where people weren't trying to kill each other. King Kona's family owned a dive shop on the Big Island. Going there for a few days could be a nice break. Billy always bragged about the weather, the diving, and how great his family was. Of course his sisters would be off-limits. A guy didn't hook up with a buddy's sister; that was an unbreakable code. But Brooklyn couldn't wrap his mind around the idea of lying under a palm tree and watching the coconuts fall.

Conway sat back and steepled his fingers under his chin. "My wife and I are booked on a cruise, but her mother has decided now would be a good time to have the knee replacement surgery she's been putting off for two years. Martha won't leave her mother. We're supposed to sail Thursday afternoon. Thirteen nights. Too late for a refund. You'd have the cabin to yourself."

"I can't—"

"You'd be doing me a favor. If you take my place, I can pass the bill on to accounting. Otherwise I have to eat the cost."

Thirteen days of poolside lounging. The Hawaiian coconuts were looking more appealing. Except… ship pools had babes in bikinis. After two years in another world, he wouldn't object to skipping Rest and going directly for Recreation. "Okay. I'll do it. But you'll owe me."

Conway's lips tipped up in a much-too-satisfied grin.

Somewhere deep down in his gut Luke was sure he'd just been had.

CHAPTER TWO

"Stop!"

Luke froze as a three-foot-high whirlwind whizzed by, an exasperated mother trotting along behind the little boy. Though she might have made better progress apprehending the wayward kid if she'd put a little more speed into her stride.

Not far behind her, two older people—a man with a waistline broad enough to hide the whole family and a short gray-haired woman with glasses that ate up half her face—strolled after the mother and child. Their prideful grins could only mean they'd begotten the woman incapable of keeping up with her charge.

Glancing around the promenade level, Luke finally got Conway's joke. Luke had stumbled over and around enough pre–baby boomers since boarding the ship to populate a metropolitan city. As far as he could tell, the only single unattached female passengers to be found on this ship had yet to attend kindergarten.

When the hell had *The Love Boat* become *Everyone Loves Raymond*?

At least Conway had good taste and had booked a cabin with a balcony. And, from the looks of it, the sound of the ocean at night through the open sliding door might be the only comfort Luke would get on this cruise.

"Excuse me." A short, slight woman—old enough to be his grandmother, or at least his mom's big sister—stood holding a soft ice cream cone in each hand. "Have you seen my granddaughter? She was here just a moment ago."

"What does she look like?"

"Pretty thing. Has on a blue sundress. I told her I'd be

right back. I don't want to miss the launch party poolside. Will you be going?"

That was the plan. He'd been checking out the facilities—and the women, or lack thereof—on his way to the upper deck.

"Oh, excuse me." A tall redhead with boobs up to her neck almost tripped over the old lady dripping ice cream at his side. "So sorry."

It took Luke all of two seconds to assess the boob job and a rock the size of Gibraltar on her left-hand ring finger before she took off. Some slightly over-the-hill banker had probably paid for the ring—and the boobs.

"You're good." The silver-haired woman smiled up at him. "I'm impressed."

"Beg your pardon?"

"Your eyes barely moved. How long did it take you? Three seconds? Maybe two?"

The old bird was on the ball. He wouldn't have expected a woman of her age to be so observant. "Two," he answered.

"Any idea how many carats she was flashing?"

"No, ma'am."

The woman's eyes twinkled with amusement.

He had a feeling she wasn't looking for information so much as testing him. If she needed advice on a jewelry purchase, she was asking the wrong guy. Now, the boob job? Definitely a double D. Thirty-six.

Less than one hour on the boat and already Sharla had lost her grandmother. When Sharla had envisioned the inside of a cruise ship, she'd drawn upon images from reruns of *The Love Boat*. Five smiling crew members greeting a handful of passengers strolling through a pretty lobby. Nowhere had she imagined four thousand people on a floating city. Since only two of the ten interior decks crossed the ship, like a freeway in rush hour, they were the paths most of those four thousand people used to get back and forth. She might have to put her grandmother on a leash to keep track of her.

According to the daily program they'd found in their cabin, the band would be playing poolside at 5:00 p.m. this afternoon while the ship set sail. Nana had mentioned wanting to be there, so Sharla jabbed the Up button for the elevator. If she couldn't find her grandmother on this deck, maybe she would find her poolside. Waiting for one of four elevators, she glanced at the heavyset man in a motorized wheelchair with his smiling chubby wife—and turned toward the stairs. *Use it or lose it.*

Too many of her other parts weren't being used since Danny died, but she could still use her legs. And if she wanted to continue to see her toes in her old age when she looked down, she should make climbing the stairs a habit at the hospital too. The moment Sharla stepped through the sliding doors onto the eleventh-floor deck, the out-of-place sounds of a steel drum calypso band wafted over her. With every step she felt lighter. Freer. Ready to conquer new worlds.

"I ate your ice cream."

Out of the throngs of people following the Caribbean sounds like the Pied Piper, Nana appeared almost magically in front of her.

"It was delicious."

Ice Cream? "What ice cream?"

"I told you to wait a moment while I detoured to the ice cream machine. Maybe you're the one who needs hearing aids."

And wasn't that another bone of contention? Did she or didn't she? Only her hairdresser—and granddaughter— knew for sure. Though every so often Sharla wondered if the problem was one of selective hearing. Danny had that problem. He could hear a mouse eating cheese in the other room, but, during a football game, Sharla could have used a bullhorn, and he wouldn't hear a word she'd said until the commercial. She had yet to decide which was the case with Sophia Garibaldi.

Her grandmother slipped through the crowds with

nimble ease and leaned against the rail. "I met a nice man while I was looking for you."

This same tired tune Nana kept singing was getting old. "I don't need a nice man."

"Yes, you do, but, as it happens, I wasn't thinking of you. Herbie is a bit too experienced for a young thing like you."

There was no way Sharla was letting her mind think about how much experience Herbie or her grandmother might have—at anything.

"You know"—her grandmother kept her gaze on the skyline—"it wouldn't hurt you to have a little fun too."

"I thought you already decided Herbie was too mature for me." Sharla bit back a smile. A chance to tease Nana was irresistible.

"This is a big boat. There has to be at least one fun-worthy young man for you to pass the time with. We are going to be on this ship for almost two weeks."

"I have a month's worth of reading to catch up on. I'll be spending my spare time getting friendly with a deck lounge chair."

"If I were you, I'd rather get friendly with the fellow I bumped into on the promenade deck."

"I doubt his wife would appreciate it." The majority of passengers seemed to already be paired off and, not surprisingly during the school year, fell into one of a few categories—retirees, newlyweds or younger couples with small children.

"Not married." Sophia continued to stare ahead.

From the age of five, Sophia Garibaldi had been trained to pick the mark. Even as little as ten years ago, Sharla wouldn't have questioned her grandmother's assessment, but, now at age seventy-five, Nana's conclusions were more likely just wishful thinking.

"You doubt me?" This time Sophia turned to her granddaughter. "No ring, no tan lines, no bulge from home cooking, no settled-down man flab. As a matter of fact, with abs like his, he's either a bodybuilder or military. But the way he sized up the bimbo redhead in two seconds, I'm saying military. Single, well-trained military."

Great. First day on the cruise and not only was her grandmother already on a matchmaking mission but the woman was picking out a serviceman. Sharla had done that already. Danny had been an MP in the army and, after his four years, had joined the police force. Three years ago his luck ran out in a dark alley with a junkie too strung out to shoot straight, and yet the crackhead still managed to get off a fatal shot.

Next time Sharla walked down the aisle, if she ever did marry again, her new husband was going to have a nice safe career. A teacher. Or baker. Maybe a plumber or dry cleaner. But no policeman, no fireman and absolutely no military man.

The departure fanfare had been about as expected. Plenty of loud music and a crush of people hanging over the rail or already sprawled out in poolside lounge chairs. Before the ship had even left port, half the passengers had stripped down to swimsuits and staked a claim on their piece of deckside landscape.

It hadn't taken Luke long to decide not to eat in the dining room this evening. Conway and his wife had booked a private table for two there, which meant Luke would have been eating alone. Something he'd anticipated rectifying quickly but wasn't so sure anymore. The few eye-catching women he'd wandered past today all wore rocks the size of Manhattan on their left hands. A gaggle of giggling teens had sauntered by, stopping to give him that "holy hotness" look women in foreign ports so often flashed at the sailors with American accents. Some of the girls would no doubt grow into jaw-dropping knockouts, just not before the end of this cruise.

The ship touted some nightspots. After a quick supper he sat a while at the sports bar. Even if many of the men were collecting a pension, sports were sports. He could talk baseball with anyone, as long as they were Yankee fans. Or willing to convert.

By midnight he'd had enough scotch and ESPN. A handful of guys his age stuck around after their wives had turned in for the night, but so far Luke had found no comrade in arms in search of a good time. The club he'd scoped out shortly after departure held a great deal of promise if it were anyplace other than senior citizen–ville. It was dark, with secluded booths, soft music and—despite the barfworthy Middle Ages decor of triangles and armored suits—the place had great potential for a romantic end to a night.

The problem remained one of passenger demographics. At midnight two couples sat intertwined in secluded booths. And less than a handful of women huddled in pairs along the bar. While old enough to avoid jailbait, but not yet old enough to drink, these girls were most definitely too young for him.

It looked like Conway was going to get his wish. Whether Luke liked it or not, he was going to get plenty of rest on this blasted tin can.

CHAPTER THREE

Vacation or not, an early morning workout was pivotal to staying mission-ready. Even for the spooks. And while Luke had expected anyplace named the Shipshape Center to be dolled up for all the vacationing fitness lovers—determined to exercise off the constant flow of food and ten pounds of daily desserts—he hadn't expected a Greek sonnet. Artificial stone pillars supporting a pergola covered in twines of fake ivy in the entryway was almost enough to turn him on his heel and take him back to his room. Or maybe he could simply jump overboard and swim to shore.

"How ya goin'?"

Luke blinked. Interesting juxtaposition. Greco-Roman trappings and now an Aussie accent.

"Ya okay? Need some help, mate?"

"Thought I'd get in a little workout this morning."

"Goodo. Let me know if you need anything."

"Will do." Luke dragged his gaze past the architectural nightmare before him to the equipment fanned about the room. At the front of the ship the majority of the treadmills faced the ocean expanse. Not a bad place to run ten miles, though he'd prefer the beach. Soft sand was the best for keeping fit. Especially at his age. Soon he'd be given a desk and a *thank you very much*. Pulled off the field and relegated to merely pushing paper. Not something he cared to dwell on.

If he couldn't run on the beach, at least he could watch the ocean. The phone in his pocket set to the mood music he and the guys used for parties—favorites like John Meyer, Kenny Chesney and Jimmy Buffet—he stepped onto the center machine. Legs splayed on either side of the belt, he hit Quick Start, set the speed, increased the incline and hopped onto the rolling tread. At this easy pace he could run all day, but the display screen would let him know when he'd hit ten miles.

Almost an hour later Luke moved on to heavy weights, surprised to see the place filling up. From the way some of the women used the machinery, he could tell these were no cruise ship fitness newbies. And considering some were likely old enough to be his mother, they were in fine shape.

"Here ya go now." The Aussie personal trainer stepped across the weights area with a rather attractive-looking blonde beside him.

A quick review noted she wasn't wearing a ring, but few people wore jewelry for working out.

The young trainer rolled out an exercise ball, leaned back on it and—with his knees bent, feet forward and shoulders resting on the large globe—demonstrated lifting three-pound dumbbells in each hand up in the air and back down to his chest. With each rep, as the man held his hips horizontal to the ground and balanced with only his shoulders on the ball, the pretty blonde's eyes grew larger and larger.

Apparently Luke had found his cruise ship exercise newbie.

Focused back on his own routine, Luke only sporadically glanced at the woman going through her first weight training session. He could hear the Aussie's gentle encouragement. The guy was good. Knew his stuff. But a drill sergeant he'd never be. Way too nice and patient.

With every lift of his heavy barbells, Luke wondered what was her story. The ship hadn't been at sea long enough for the blonde to worry about putting on the pounds. And, what little he saw of her curves, they seemed to be in all the right places. Maybe she could see the signs of her moneybags husband getting ready to move on to the next trophy wife. Luke cast a quick casual glance in her direction again. Definitely did not have that strictly arm-candy look about her. If anything she looked capable of making commercials for Dove soap or Ivory Snow. There was more to having a wholesome image than simply not wearing makeup. This woman had wholesome written all over her.

Another rep and the trainer called enough, moving his client out of the weights area and across the fitness center out of view. Too bad. By the time Luke finished, the blonde was nowhere to be seen.

Two steps into the hall, Luke almost plowed over the same little old lady he'd run into the day before with the ice creams. "Lost your granddaughter again?"

"As a matter of fact, yes." She shook her head. "She was supposed to join me for morning trivia and never showed."

"Trivia?"

"You any good at it? We could use some younger input. Best teams always have an age mix. I've got down the stuff of ancient history books. If Sharla comes, she's good at science, but she's not likely to have any idea what color shirt is worn by the leader in the Tour de France."

He didn't know why but something about this old bird was quite captivating. A mischievous twinkle gleamed in her marble-blue eyes.

"Yellow," he supplied.

The glimmer brightened to the level of a Fourth of July sparkler. "I knew it. Two thirty this afternoon. Afternoon trivia. Leeward Lounge. I'll save you a seat!"

Before Luke could process the order, never mind respond, the woman scampered off like a kid after a new kitten. Instead of being annoyed, all he could do was smile. He hadn't planned on spending his vacation playing trivia with a spry granny, but, so far, she was the most interesting action he'd come across. Besides, SEALs like to win. If the grandkid was any good at her schoolwork, how hard could it be to out-trivia a bar full of senior-citizen Jeopardy enthusiasts?

Holy biceps. Sharla leaned back against the cabin door and sucked in a lungful of much-needed air. The minute she'd spotted the guy on the weight bench, she'd lost her breath and had never quite recovered. A time or two she thought she'd noticed him looking in her direction but finally decided it had to have been her imagination. *Or wishful thinking.*

And where had that come from? She was not in the market for a man of any kind for any reason. But danged if just looking at the guy in the fitness center hadn't set her to a low simmer. Had she found the courage to brush up against him, she'd have no doubt bubbled over in a full rolling boil.

Pulling her wristwatch from her pocket, she checked the time. Almost eleven. *Shoot.* She was supposed to have met her grandmother an hour ago for morning trivia. One of the reasons Nana and Great-Aunt Leticia loved to cruise on this line was all the trivia. Sharla hadn't meant to linger at the fitness center. All she'd really wanted was a little intro information. But when Kyle had opened his mouth and that Australian accent had come out, she had instinctively followed him about like a sappy puppy. Then she'd spotted Mr. Weight Lifter and lost all track of coherent thought. And time.

Still pressed against the cabin door, Sharla felt the handle jiggle behind her back before her grandmother shoved her forward.

"I'm going to have to tie a bell around your neck, aren't I?"

"Sorry, Nana. Lost track of time."

"Hmm. I don't suppose you know what color T-shirt the leader wears in the Tour de France?"

Sharla shook her head.

"What is the largest web-footed bird?"

Sharla shrugged.

"Okay, you're forgiven. This time." Nana eased past her granddaughter. "Are we having lunch in the dining room or upstairs in the cafeteria?"

"Do you have a preference?"

Nana studied the daily schedule in her hand. "No, so long as I'm not late for the Sexiest Man competition poolside at one o'clock."

Sexiest Man? On this ship? Sharla wasn't sure if she should laugh or cry. "Maybe we'd better do the upstairs buffet just in case. Give me ten minutes to shower and change, and we can head up."

A highlighter in one hand, Nana sank onto her bed still studying the schedule.

Sexiest Man Contest. What was her grandmother thinking? Grabbing a short-sleeve shirt and tan shorts from the closet, Sharla's thoughts shifted to the sweat-covered muscles of Mr. Weight Lifter. Now *that* was sexy. Even she wouldn't mind hurrying through lunch if it meant another glimpse of that eye candy. Stepping into the phone-booth-size shower, Sharla had to admit, maybe her grandmother had the right idea after all about having fun on this trip.

The minute Luke crossed into the back portion of the cafeteria, the bitter smell of burned rubber slapped him in the face.

"Smells like the cook stepped away from the stove," a nearby passenger said, then laughed.

"Or fried his shoes," another added, scooping up several cookies from the dessert island.

Dish already in hand, Luke scanned the immediate area, searching for fire extinguishers and alarms. His eyes quickly surveyed the walls for outlets and sparks. The smell—growing stronger—had nothing to do with overcooked lunch.

Plastic grates formed the ceiling that hid the wiring for the lights and the pipes for the sprinkler system. At least if the place went up in flames, the sprinklers would kick in before any serious damage could be done.

Of course one of the first things he'd learned in basic training was to never count on *if.*

Waiters in Hawaiian shirts meandered about. Cooks in high white hats flipped burgers and filled salad bowls, but not a single member of the staff had their nose to the air in search of the source of the nasty odor.

Where the heck was the source?

Giving up all pretense of being a hungry passenger in search of food, Luke set aside his plate and, not spotting electrical outlets on the walls, focused his attention on the grated ceilings where he could see all the wiring and fixtures above.

Somewhere…

Flash…

Sparks splattered like holiday fireworks. Pointing to the fixture at ten o'clock, Luke turned to the nearest cook and hollered, "Fire. Turn off the lights."

Like a scared rabbit, the little guy turned tail and ran into the kitchen.

Expecting him to come running out any second with a fire extinguisher, Luke was taken aback to not only see that the lights were still on but to have a second cook stroll out of the kitchen, glancing about as though searching for an empty seat in a crowded restaurant.

This was not good.

A slender middle-aged woman—with a nose that could probably have sniffed out drug smugglers—let out an ear-shattering screech. "Fire!"

Luke could envision it now. Five hundred people trampling their way past the fire brigade in a mad dash to jump overboard. "Let's clear the way, everyone. Nice and easy. Move along."

The waiters actually had the nerve to give him a dirty look, while cook number three made an appearance through the galley entry, and the small fire flashed across the wire to the corner in another burst of flames.

Clearly no one had any intention of dealing with the problem at hand. Luke grabbed the nearest employee in blue pants and a white shirt, which hopefully meant the guy was some kind of lunchroom supervisor. "Get everyone out of here. Do not let them panic."

Brows buckled in confusion, the idiot didn't move.

Luke pointed to the fire in the ceiling and shouted, "Now." Relieved to see the man's eyes widen as he called for his staff to clear the restaurant, Luke waited expectantly. And still no alarms sounded, no sprinklers kicked on and no extinguishers were brought in.

Talk about FUBAR. If the sailors on board a navy vessel took this long to find a fire extinguisher, Uncle Sam wouldn't have any ships left to sail. Enough was enough. Working his way past the slow-exiting passengers still adding food to their plates—apparently missing lunch was a fate worse than getting trapped by a fire—Luke ignored the befuddled staff huddled by the doorway and stormed into the galley.

Seriously? Three paces to his right. In front of everyone. Bright red with black letters. He grabbed the CO_2 extinguisher designated for Class B electrical fires that no one else seemed to be able to find, and pushed past the kitchen crew now muttering in broken English and other miscellaneous dialects.

Below the fire, Luke positioned the discharge horn, broke the safety seal and pulled out the pin. Holding the base, he tested the discharge and, squeezing the handle, moved closer to the fire source. When the yellow and red licks of flame smothered to nothing, he backed away, released the handle and set down the canister.

Turning around in the now smoke-filled room, Luke found himself surrounded by uniforms.

A wall of men with arms crossed, brows furrowed and none too happy.

"Oops."

CHAPTER FOUR

"Hurry up. I want a good seat poolside."

"What seat?" Sharla followed her grandmother. "Every passenger on the ship has to be on deck." This morning on her way to the fitness center, Sharla had been surprised to see so many deck chairs already occupied. She loved the sun as much as the next guy, but some of those people must have been up at the crack of dawn to reserve their spot.

"Always glass half empty." Her grandmother shook her head and eased her way ahead of Sharla to the open area by the pool, then looked around at the—as predicted—occupied chairs.

Her fingers to her forehead, Nana dramatically wiped nonexistent sweat from her brow, and the hairs on Sharla's neck prickled with awareness. *She couldn't.*

Slowing her gait, Nana walked from one deck chair to another, holding on to the backs like a railing.

She wouldn't. Sharla picked up her pace in an effort to catch up with her grandmother.

Pausing behind a chair with a middle-aged man reading a paperback, Nana scanned the area, and…

Crap. *She did.*

Like a two-ton anvil, Sophia Garibaldi dropped to the ground with a well-practiced thud.

Any hopes Sharla might have had of reaching her grandmother first faded into oblivion as a crowd of sunbathers swarmed the little old lady gracefully sprawled across the deck. If nothing else, Sharla had to give her grandmother credit. The woman knew how to take a dive.

"Excuse me." Sharla pushed through the growing group

of onlookers. "That's my grandmother."

Few people moved.

Sharla had never learned the art of slithering through a crowd undetected. That skill had ended a generation before with her mom. Though trained in the family business, Sharla's mother had fallen in love and followed the straight-and-narrow, if not somewhat nomadic, lifestyle of Sharla's archeologist father.

Once in a while one of the old-timers in the family would try to teach Sharla some of the arts, but Nana didn't want to upset her son-in-law and risk being banned from visiting Sharla. Especially when she reached school age, and her mom would go off with her dad on some expedition or other and leave Sharla with Nana.

The cruise ship version of poolside Muzak came to an abrupt stop. "Alpha, alpha, alpha. Midship pool, deck eleven. Alpha, alpha, alpha."

Double crap. Sharla had no idea what the code word *alpha* meant, but she did understand *pool, deck eleven*. The cavalry was being called out for her con-artist grandmother. Marvelous.

Finally squeezing between the last two oversize passengers between her and her grandmother, Sharla was able to see up close how pale the old woman looked. A sudden sense of panic raced from her stomach and gripped her by the throat. Could the collapse have been real? Was her spunky seventy-five-year-old grandmother not as healthy as Sharla had thought?

Propelled by fear for her beloved Nana, Sharla shoved aside the samurai-sized passenger still in her way and stood at her grandmother's feet. Dropping to the ground, Sharla studied Nana quickly.

Another passenger had his fingers on Nana's neck while staring at the watch on his other arm. "Probably dehydration," he muttered to no one in particular.

"Excuse me." A deep male voice sounded past the curious onlookers still hovering closely around.

Sharla glanced away from the man checking Nana's pulse to see a ship's officer slip in beside him, then, after a single glance, signal to the staff who had accompanied him. While her heart stuttered to a normal beat, she watched her grandmother carefully. No movement of any kind.

She shouldn't have been so hard on Nana. It was difficult to remember that her grandmother was reaching the end of the average life expectancy for a female living in Florida. Nana was such a feisty gal that Sharla realized she hadn't really come to grips with the idea that Nana would ever die. And Sharla certainly wasn't ready to lose her grandmother now. A multitude of possibilities flipped through Sharla's mind, from a ministroke to a massive coronary and everything in between. Her mouth totally dry, she was unable to swallow back her fears. If Nana had merely passed out from the heat, she should have come to by now. Dang it. Why was she still out cold?

And then Sharla saw it. Not much. But she suddenly remembered the tell. The double tap of an otherwise unnoticed pinkie. The old biddy was faking it. For a dumb deck chair.

The moment two of the ship's staff returned with a gurney, Nana's eyes miraculously fluttered open. Her dazed and confused look was worthy of an Academy Award.

"What happened?"

The ship's doctor checked her pulse under the watchful eye of the passenger physician in a Speedo.

There should be laws about mature men in Speedos.

"You passed out. What's your name?"

"Sophia. Sophia Garibaldi."

The doc glanced at Sharla and waited for her confirming nod. "Very good, Sophia. How many fingers am I holding up?"

Nana had the audacity to squint and strain before answering, "The sun's in my eyes, but I see two."

"That's right." The man took hold of her wrist and turned to his watch. "What did you have for breakfast?"

"Coffee and a muffin."

Sharla almost laughed in her grandmother's face. Nana had eaten a specialty three-egg omelet with bacon, sausage and a side of French toast. The woman's metabolism was the envy of every over-thirty female on the Eastern Seaboard.

"I suspect you're dehydrated, but it would be a good idea to come to sick bay for a quick checkup."

"No." Nana patted her heart and, circling her gaze over the people still hovering, offered a meager smile. "I'm sure I'd be all right if I could just have some water and a few minutes to rest."

The ship's physician and Dr. Speedo both bobbed their heads. Though the thin press of the ship doctor's lips told Sharla that he was wondering what the odds were of having Nana back in his care.

If he only knew.

Meanwhile a handful of bystanders waved down a waiter to order a bottled water.

The man—whose chair Nana had carefully chosen to collapse nearby—retrieved his paperback and other belongings as well as those of his companion, then gestured for Nana to take his place.

All these years and Nana could still pick the mark. Now Sharla and Nana both had prime seats for the upcoming outdoor activities. But as soon as they were back in their cabin, Sharla was going to kill her grandmother.

Luke took in the grimacing faces. They acted as if he'd set the fire instead of putting it out.

"Alpha, alpha, alpha. Midship pool, deck eleven. Alpha, alpha, alpha." The words boomed through the PA system. All eyes shifted focus from him to the speakers embedded in the ceiling.

When the emergency call ceased, the captain sucked in a deep breath. "What's your name?"

"Lieutenant Luke Chapman." He resisted the urge to stand at attention and left off the parts about being a former SEAL team leader and now working as a State Department employee. A well-known euphemism for *CIA agent.*

"Navy." The way the man huffed the word on a tired breath, *navy* sounded like a four-letter word of a different kind. Though certified up the wazoo to run these massive vessels, most cruise ship captains came from commercial maritime backgrounds, not military. And this one didn't seem any too pleased with Luke's naval background. "I'll deal with you later."

By now the fire brigade had arrived. Men scurried, opened fire closets, tussled equipment about. And more than a few engineers scrambled to assure the fire was completely out and the problem under control.

The captain and a couple of the other sour faces took off toward the exit from the now roped-off eating area. Two men in uniform remained behind.

The one shouting orders—in what Luke thought to be a French accent of some sort—was clearly the man who knew what was going on.

A quick glance at the country on the name tag confirmed French-Canadian. With everyone distracted, Luke thought this as good a chance as any to slip away and let the Keystone Kops do their thing.

"Lieutenant." Frenchy turned toward Luke.

"Yes." He hadn't expected the respect of rank. He almost smiled.

"Not that there will be a next time, but, just in case, please resist any more urges to play hero. Our staff is very well trained."

Clearly Luke's definition of *well trained* and the ship's second officer's were not the same, but Luke agreed with the man anyway.

"And…" Frenchy looked to the burned ceiling grate and back. "Thank you."

This time Luke let himself grin, just a bit. He still had little faith in the emergency training of the kitchen staff, but he had a feeling that not much got past the man in charge now. Though a small consolation on a one-hundred-thousand-ton ship, at least Luke wouldn't feel the need to sleep with one eye open.

Since lunch had been so rudely interrupted, and most of

the crowd were funneling their way downstairs to the main dining rooms, he chose the lesser-traveled path to the soda shop across from the upper pool deck. Careful to avoid the captain en route, Luke slipped inside and instantly felt transported back in time. He wouldn't have been surprised in the least to see Richie from the retro TV show *Happy Days* come out to greet him. Even Bill Haley's "Rock Around the Clock" played in the background. A stark contrast to the calypso music on deck or the Latin rhythms at the atrium bar.

Taking in his options, he ordered a chili dog with the works. Across from the cashier, a row of glass windows looked down on the poolside activities. Luke opted for sliding onto a stool and chowing down while observing the masses from on high.

Blaring instructions through a speaker system that made a megaphone sound like high definition, the cruise director called the guests to order.

At least for the guy's sake, Luke hoped the sound system was to blame for the quality of his voice and that the announcer's name wasn't really Insk from Minsk.

The people at the outer edges of the deck slowly rose from their seats and circled in closer to center stage.

Pulling out his copy of the day's activities, Luke scrolled down to the current time to find out what he was watching. "World's Sexiest Man Contest." Roaring laughter burst through from deep in his gut.

"Just wait, mate. It gets worse." A familiar voice came from behind. The trainer from the fitness center took a seat beside him.

"How is that?"

"Ya have to see."

Insk lined up four women in deck chairs along the back wall by the end of the pool. Then he called for the contestants.

Luke wasn't sure how the group had been gathered, but each man strutted like an arrogant peacock. Short and firm and about seventy with a thick head of white hair, the first guy strolled past the women. "Silver Fox," Luke muttered, assigning the old codger a call sign.

Apparently the band or DJ had a sense of humor because "I'm Too Sexy" played loudly while the old geezer flexed and posed for each of the women.

Next was a younger guy who had spent way too many hours at the *bierhaus*. That or he was due to give birth any week now. Comfortable in a swimsuit that barely covered what Mother Nature had given him, he gyrated and bucked, pausing briefly in front of each lady to the tune of "Macho Man."

Luke thought "Having My Baby" might have been more appropriate. "I see what you mean."

"Keep an eye on the old broad. They're the ones ya have to look out for."

"Thanks." Luke stuck out his hand. "Brooklyn."

The Aussie raised a brow and shook his hand. "Kyle."

Luke focused on the four judges. The "old broad" Kyle had referred to was none other than the lady constantly in search of her missing grandchild and very likely the head honcho of his trivia team. "What exactly am I looking for?"

No sooner had the words fallen from his lips than a young buck, with tattoos covering more skin than not, ground and spun his way to the beat of "It's Raining Men." When he got to Granny, who was practically out of her seat with enthusiasm, he paused and bucked and…

Luke leaned in for a better view. "Did she just—"

"Pinch his arse? Righto. Last cruise some old bag grabbed the guy's package and had no mind to let go. Don't let their age fool ya. These sheilas have no fun filters."

"Fun filters?"

"I've had many a bruised backside. But ya learn not to turn your back on 'em, and when ya do—move bloody fast." Kyle gathered his empty drink and dirty napkin onto the paper plate. "Got to bolt. Stay safe."

Curious, Luke kept his gaze on the old lady but shot Kyle a thumbs-up. This woman was something else. She'd hold up both hands and, curling her forefingers, would call to the better-built candidates. And if Luke wasn't completely mistaken, he got the impression that the old bird had slipped a folded piece of paper into one gyrator's waistband. Granny was definitely a firecracker.

CHAPTER FIVE

"**M**y God, Nana." Sharla tossed her e-reader onto the extra chair in the Leeward Lounge and waived a bartender over to their table. "I'll have a piña colada, please."

"And I'll have—"

"She'll have a cola."

Nana crossed her arms and glared at her granddaughter, but Sharla didn't care. The last thing her grandmother needed now was liquid courage. Sharla, on the other hand, would probably have to drink a barrel of rum before she'd shake off the embarrassment. "Really, Nana. First you do a swan dive just to get a deck chair. Then you ignored the contest judges' *no touching* rules and pinched Tattoo Man's rear. But what were you thinking slipping a ten-dollar bill in the last contestant's Speedo?" Maybe Sharla should have ordered a scotch.

"Don't forget my room number."

Sharla sucked in a breath and hoped her eyes didn't pop out of their sockets. "You slipped him our cabin number?"

Nana shrugged. "Nothing ventured, nothing gained."

The waiter returned with their drinks, and Sharla took a long slurp from the straw. If she was lucky, she'd suffer permanent brain freeze.

"Ready to play, ladies?" An older gentleman in plaid shorts, a flowered shirt, white socks and brown sandals sank into the nearest chair.

Standard Florida-retiree uniform.

Despite Nana's earlier brazen antics, her cheeks flushed a pale pink, and her expression turned coy and bashful.

Sharla blinked and gave the visitor a second look.

"Sweetie, this is Herbie." Nana gestured toward the man. "You remember I mentioned him."

Sharla forced a smile. Odds were he was a very nice man, but she still hadn't recovered from the poolside escapades and moving on to a new beau for her grandmother wasn't going to work until Sharla had had a stronger drink.

"Your grandmother speaks of you with much love," he said.

A heartfelt smile overtook Sharla's previous plastic grin. "The feeling is mutual." And it was. She couldn't imagine her world without her crazy grandmother. Well, maybe a slightly calmer world wasn't too hard to picture.

The empty chairs in the lounge slowly began to fill up. As the seats disappeared, newcomers joined forces with folks who had an extra chair or two. Four ladies—wearing red hats and purple bathing suit cover-ups on the other side of the grand piano—kept Sharla's attention. She'd heard of the Red Hat Society but had never actually been anywhere among its members. Judging by the number of women running about donning red hats, they must be having a conference of some kind on board.

Two of the ladies, laughing at nothing in particular, were likely close to Nana's age. Another looked to be somewhere in the required age group to wear the signature millinery, but the last one didn't look old enough to be a member, yet the floppy wide-brimmed red hat she wore said she was at least fifty. Tall, slim, with shapely legs and ample cleavage.

Sharla should look so good now, never mind in another twenty years.

"Excuse me."

A strong male voice dragged Sharla's attention away from the table of laughing ladies.

"You made it!" Nana sprang from her seat and nearly hopped over Herbie to sidle up next to the man.

The voice may have caught Sharla's attention, but seeing the Adonis from the gym stole her breath. Flat on his back, she'd had a general idea of his good-looking assets, but, on his feet, he was heart-stoppingly handsome. He looked to be close to six foot, with broad shoulders, a stone wall of a chest and a Hollywood-trim waist. But the toned muscles on this man screamed Greek god, not movie star make-believe.

"Herbie"—Nana linked an arm with the older man now standing at her side—"this is the young man I mentioned."

"Herbie Klein." The older man stuck out his hand.

"Luke Chapman. I'll also answer to Brooklyn."

Herbie bit back a smile. "I understand you're going to be our trivia secret weapon."

The corner of Luke's lips curved up in a grin that lit up his face.

Holy cow. Where was this man's wife? And what was she doing letting him out loose on his own? Nana had been sticking ten-dollar bills down the wrong swim trunks.

"I don't know about that, sir."

"Herbie. Please."

"Herbie," Luke repeated.

"And this"—Nana elbowed Sharla in the rib cage—"is my granddaughter, Sharla."

Fine lines deepened in the corners of his eyes, making the blue centers sparkle.

If anyone had told her that one of her grandmother's strays would make her weak in the knees with just a smile, she would have laughed in their face. Peeling her tongue from the roof of her very dry mouth, Sharla stuck out her hand. "Hello."

"Is everyone ready?" A pert young brunette with her dark hair in a ponytail smiled at the crowd. "I'm Becky on your cruise director's staff." She rattled off instructions for how to play the game as representatives from each team stepped forward to get paper and pencil to participate.

Delighted to have been saved from opening mouth and inserting foot, Sharla settled back in her seat.

As Becky asked the first question, a couple hurried into the lounge and stood dead center. The redhead circled the room with her gaze, while her husband's search stopped at the bar. The guy was either bored, indifferent or not terribly sharp.

Sharla was betting on door number two.

Unlike the thirsty husband, both men at Sharla's table kept their eyes glued to the endowed redhead now moving toward them.

"Could we join your team?"

Sharla was convinced had the woman tipped half an inch closer, her boobs would have spilled out onto Luke's lap. But Sharla had to give him credit. His eyes remained fixed on the buxom redhead's face. Apparently his self-control matched his superior physical conditioning, because even Danny would have taken at least a small peek at the goodies offered.

For a split second Nana frowned, then a bright smile slipped into place. "Of course. The more the merrier."

Nana took her trivia seriously. And she had certain rules. A second sheet of paper and pencil were required for notes, since no one could actually speak a response that a nearby team might overhear. Another piece of paper was required to cover the answer sheet. Just in case the hundred-year-old woman ten feet away had bionic eyes. And of course, in control of the official pencil, Nana had the last word on the correct answers.

The bored husband kept trying to strike up a conversation with Herbie. Nana, having none of it, tapped her pencil and dragged both men into the game.

It didn't take long to see why Nana had been so enthused about the guy from the gym joining them. So far he'd been the only one to know that an aircraft carrier is the largest ship in a naval fleet, that Floyd Mayweather is the highest paid athlete in the world and that 5:00 p.m. is the traditional hour for a bullfight to begin.

Sharla finally had a chance to contribute when the next trivia question wanted to know what was the more recognizable name for the chemical compound sildenafil citrate. To her surprise neither of the older men at the table came up with *Viagra*.

When it came time to trade papers for scoring, there was only one question their team truly pulled a guess out of a hat for. *What was Ed Sullivan's wife's name?* Once that shot in the dark was added to their official answer sheet, Nana then scribbled the words *Guys and Dolls* across the paper for her team's name and handed it over to the folks at the nearest table.

The game had proven to be a good distraction for Sharla. Her heart rate had returned to normal, and saliva had returned to her mouth. Of course the second piña colada might have helped. As did keeping her gaze anywhere but on Luke Chapman.

Waiting for Becky, the staff person, to begin the answer round, Nana pulled out her schedule. She wore her room card around her neck clipped to a blinged-out necklace that could start a fire on a sunny day. Tucked in the back of the plastic case holding the keycard, she kept the daily schedule. Highlighted, circled and checked often, the data was her vacation bible. Having already looked at the paper a hundred times today, Nana consulted the page one more time. Sharla couldn't imagine what Nana expected to find that she hadn't already seen.

Paper in hand, Nana leaned forward. "Tell me, Luke, do you have plans for this evening at eight?"

One brow rose high on his forehead, and a wide grin took over his face. He leaned in as well. "What did you have in mind, Sophia?"

Even Big Red turned at Luke's husky voice that warmed a girl from the inside out like a smooth aged whiskey.

"Tonight's music trivia is the eighties. I'd be delighted if you graced us with your presence again."

"Absolutely, Sophia."

"Good." Nana gave one brisk nod and looked to Becky, ready to move on. Everyone anxious to finish the game.

Except Sharla was pretty sure she was going to need a lot more liquid strength to get through two weeks of *games* while sitting next to Nana's new best friend.

For the first time since the trivia contest had started, Luke's and Sharla's gazes caught, and he smiled at her.

Oh, yeah. Lots of liquid strength.

CHAPTER SIX

Something wasn't right. Luke felt it in his bones. The minute the redhead with the Double Ds had walked in, Herbie had grown stiff and serious. He'd made every effort to shake it off, to be cordial, but Luke could smell a rat.

And he didn't have to be a guru of observation to know Mr. Double D was no banker. Not the legal kind. Totally unconcerned with the trivia game, the man only showed a hint of social skills when the chance of any conversation with Herbie had flared. From what Luke could decipher, the man seemed quite charming. Reminded Luke of the snake oil salesmen of old.

The pert brunette with the East London accent read the first correct response, and Sophia squealed with delight, marking a big X in front of the neighboring team's answer. Sophia had been the one to insist that *From Here to Eternity* was the movie to win Frank Sinatra the coveted Academy Award.

Luke had known the answer as well. But his information came more from a love of all trivia associated with *The Godfather* movies than to any interest in Frank Sinatra. Though the crooner did produce awfully good mood music.

Sophia squealed again, rubbing her hands together. Her smile was so big and bright, she could put the Cheshire cat out of business.

And Luke loved it. It had been a long time since the urge to smile had overtaken him. The last two and a half years had been deep and dark and dirty.

By now Mrs. Double D and the granddaughter were

building enthusiasm as well. The two women provided a great deal of contrast. The one as plastic as a credit card, the other as natural as a summer breeze. From his encounters with Sophia, he'd expected her granddaughter to be a geeky teen who loved ice cream and studied advanced-placement biology, but a fully grown brown-eyed woman had never crossed his mind.

Mr. Double D was back to conversing with Herbie.

While the two men had their heads drawn closer together, Sophia ignored their conversation, her eyes and ears only for the crew staff.

A word here or there reached Luke. *Resort. Yield. Profit.* He waited for the last of the trivia answers to be shared, the corrected answer sheets to be traded back, Sophia to do a little hip jig in her seat and Sharla to do the same before sharing a hearty high-five with her grandmother. She had the same spunk as Sophia. His grin grew wider.

Drawn out of their tête-à-tête by the hand slapping and laughter, Mr. Double D, whose name Luke had yet to learn, and Herbie joined in the celebration. Though Luke suspected the snake oil salesman was more enthused about his progress with Herbie than the key chain prizes Sophia had just happily collected.

Giddy with winning, despite not having known Ed Sullivan's wife was Sylvie, Sophia hugged each of the team members. Sharla hung on extra long to her grandmother before turning to the redhead, Herbie and then… him.

For all of five seconds Sharla molded into him like a comfortable feather pillow. He'd barely gotten his arms around her waist when the redhead slid against him for her turn. An unexpected sense of loss overtook him as Sharla pulled away. Their gazes had locked a moment longer than they should have, and, for just a second, he thought she seemed equally stunned. In the brief time she'd held on to him, he'd felt he'd known her forever. Had come home. Not even the press of Mrs. Double D's bought-and-paid-for superboobs against his chest could steal his thoughts away from Sharla.

Earlier he'd automatically scanned her left hand, pleased to see it remained bare. Only slightly disappointed to now notice the understated set of wedding rings on her right hand. Once again he wondered what was this woman's story. The feel of her—now seared in his memory—spiked his curiosity. What was it about this woman that had him wanting to learn all about her? Her favorite color. Her first kiss.

"I'm going to try my luck in the casino before dinner." Sophia latched the plastic cruise line key chain onto the sparkly lanyard hanging around her neck and, still sporting a broad smile, pushed to her feet. "Anyone else interested?"

The redhead shook her head, and spreading her fingers wide, announced she had an appointment at the spa.

No surprise there.

"I'm going to find a nice quiet chair on the promenade and do a little reading." Sharla scooped up a small colorful cloth pouch with a long strap and slung it over her shoulder. "Just don't spend too much money on the slots, Nana."

"Slots?" Sophia huffed softly. "I'll be shooting craps."

Herbie's brows rose with interest, and Mr. Snake Oil quickly added, "I prefer a sure thing." Then the guy leaned back and motioned for a waiter.

Smooth. Drop the hook and wait for the fish. Luke had to give Snake Oil Man credit for playing it cool.

"I'll have a scotch on the rocks," Snake Oil ordered.

"Make mine a Bud," Herbie added.

Might as well make it a triple play. "Bud for me too."

The waiter walked away, and Snake Oil leaned across the small round table between them, extending his hand to Luke. "George Bailey."

Seriously? Jimmy Stewart's George Bailey? Years of hard-core training in life-threatening situations made it easy for Luke to keep a straight face. George Bailey, the sainted friend and neighbor from the beloved movie *It's a Wonderful Life*. The man everyone trusted. The consummate big brother looking out for the little guy. Sadly the subliminal connection probably worked too well on his unsuspecting prey. "Luke Chapman."

For the next hour they talked sports, switching from the upcoming NBA championship games to MLB trades to NFL draft picks. Just a few guys hanging out over beer and pretzels. No oil for sale yet. The guy was biding his time. He had almost two weeks. Maybe Luke wasn't the right demographic. Or maybe the guy was on the up-and-up and just had the misfortune to smell like a rat.

Either way, for the next twelve days, Luke had nothing but time on his hands.

"You won how much?" Sharla's hand froze midbrushstroke.

Nana tightened the bathrobe belt, shrugged a shoulder and pulled a dress for dinner out of the closet. "Only two hundred."

Only? Sometimes Sharla worried her grandmother had too cavalier an attitude about money. Wasn't the Depression-era generation supposed to be more frugal? Although, if she thought about it, most of today's elderly seniors hadn't come from a family of grifters either. Nana making her money the hard way at the crap tables was probably a heck of a lot safer than running a con. Not that Nana had been involved in the family business over the last few decades, but her determination to keep her skills sharp by playing with marks from time to time worried the dickens out of Sharla.

The times the police had brought Nana home for returning a mark's wallet to their pocket or purse, after successfully picking her prize, were coming more frequently. How long would it be before she got caught doing the picking and not the returning? Yep, gaming tables were definitely safer.

"So what do you think about Herbie?"

"He seems nice enough."

"He does, doesn't he?" Nana slipped out of the robe and into the dress. "Just one teeny flaw."

"And what would that be?" Crossing her fingers, she

hoped her grandmother wasn't about to say something really awkward.

"He's a retired cop."

Sharla nearly choked on her own spit. Of all the "nice" men for her sticky-fingered grandmother to get friendly with. "Nana, a policeman?"

"Retired, dear. It makes a difference. And he is very nice."

There was no arguing that. Sharla had just said so herself a few moments ago, and she did like the way Nana's face glowed at the mention of Herbie. That wasn't something Sharla was used to seeing.

Grandpa Garibaldi had passed on before Sharla was born. After years of supporting his family by running some of the most complex, successful and probably dangerous long cons out there, the man had dropped dead from a brain hemorrhage when crossing a street.

Sharla wasn't sure which was worse. Having a life cut too short because of an act of nature or in the line of duty. Both sucked. Big time.

At least Nana and Grandpa had had enough years together to raise a family. Sharla and Danny hadn't reached the point of even discussing children. They'd thought time was on their side. She'd fought the tightening in her gut every time he'd walked out the door in uniform. She'd clung to the numbers. Odds were he'd live to retirement with an uneventful career. The odds had been wrong.

And now there was Luke Chapman. Not since the first time she'd laid eyes on her future husband had Sharla been so intrigued by just the sight of a man. And that brief hug. She'd felt the warmth of Luke's embrace all the way to her toes. But it was more than that. She'd felt cared for. And safe. Only a five second hug from a stranger and he'd made her feel totally safe. She liked that.

It was time to think ahead, instead of staying in the past. A nice life with a regular guy who didn't put his life on the line every day.

If Luke was going to use his connections to gather info on Good Old George, he was going to need more than a first and last name along with a list of the guy's favorite sports teams. Sophia hadn't invited the couple to join the team for the evening's entertainment, but, when George had stood to join his wife, he'd promised to see everyone here again the next day.

Tonight after supper Luke would find a quiet corner and do a little digging. See what he could come up with. If the universe was kind, George would be a real idiot and an easy takedown. If he was sharper than he looked, Luke might not be getting that rest Conway wanted him to have after all.

CHAPTER SEVEN

Eating alone in the dining room had been pretty much what Luke had expected. Fast and boring. A few nearby passengers glanced his way, then quickly averted their gazes if he caught them staring. That didn't bother him. Neither did eating alone. What did bother him was that it bothered them. Ludicrous logic but somehow he found himself feeling sorry for them wasting their nice dinners feeling sorry for him. Maybe tomorrow he'd try room service.

Nodding a silent *thank you* to the waiter and his assistant—who seemed to have made an extra effort to get Luke his food more quickly than the surrounding passengers—Luke made his way through the maze of tables to the exit doors. Noticing an older woman blatantly staring, he winked, and then, when she blushed a schoolgirl grin, he flashed her his best appreciative smile. If there's one thing he'd learned from having sisters, every woman, no matter how young or old, likes to feel pretty.

The new question was where to now? At only 7:00 p.m., he was not ready to call it a night. Besides, Sophia was expecting him for the music trivia later. Taking his time across the ship, he paused at one of the smaller lounges where the Latin trio played tunes that reminded him of warm nights on leave in Cadiz. And the Spanish beauty he'd shared them with. Now that would have been an interesting place to have returned for a vacation. Good food, good sherry and beautiful women. Everything a man could ask for. Unbidden, his thoughts immediately shifted to this afternoon's trivia game and the brief moments with Sharla in his arms. *Maybe not everything a man could ask for.*

Using the casino for a shortcut across the ship, he paused at the crap tables, almost expecting to see Sophia tossing dice and squealing with delight. A brief stop at a blackjack table had him nearly sitting to play a few rounds, but the way things had been going since he had boarded the ship, he'd probably only succeed in dropping a wad of cash. *Maybe another night.*

On the other side of the ship he found himself back at the Leeward Lounge and searching for signs of Sharla. When a couple stood up from one of the tables, he hurried to claim the spot. Ten minutes later another group stood to leave, and he commandeered one of the chairs adding a fourth seat to his table. Still unsure if George and his wife, Gloria, were joining them, Luke debated whether or not to pilfer two more chairs when Herbie came up beside him and took a seat.

"Piano player's pretty good."

Herbie was right. The guy was as good as any mainstream artist on the radio. Maybe better. "Affirmative."

"Navy?"

"Not anymore."

Herbie's brows formed a pensive V over the bridge of his nose. "I would have pegged you for career military."

"State Department."

"I see." One side of Herbie's mouth tipped up in a knowing smile.

"And you?"

"Marine Corps. Ten years. Decided I wasn't up to moving around for another ten so I signed up with Philadelphia PD."

"Is that home?"

"No. Military brat. Didn't have a home. Philly offered me a contract first, so I took it. But after twenty years I'd had enough. One day I got in my car and started driving toward warm weather. Stopped at a gas station in the middle of Nowhere, Georgia, at the same time as a couple of cocky kids from Atlanta got the bright idea that robbing a backwoods gas station would be easy. Next thing I knew, I was the chief of police, and, for the most part, the only time

I had to deal with senseless death was when I had a good catch on Lake Oconee. Retired now."

"Still in Georgia?"

"Florida. A man can only take so many years of fishing." Herbie flashed a brief smile that told Luke the old coot had probably been a catch himself in his better days.

"So you gave up your fishing boat for a cruise ship." Luke had meant the comment as a joke, but the way Herbie bristled had raised the hairs on the back of Luke's neck. He'd felt the same way a few times earlier in the day.

Before Luke could ask any more questions, Sophia came huffing through the growing crowd in the lounge and fell heavily into the chair beside Herbie.

"I thought that crazy broad—er, lady—was never going to shut up and finish her dinner." Sophia patted the curls at the back of her head and turned to Herbie. "I've asked the waiter for a new table starting tomorrow night. If we're going to make it to the evening music trivia, we can't be waiting for Ms. Chatterbox to stop gabbing long enough to eat her dinner so that the waiters will serve the rest of us our desserts."

"At least you have someone to talk with. One couple hasn't shown up yet for any dinner, and the other one is so old I feel like a young boy in short pants. But they do smile a lot." Herbie gave a short chuckle and placed the slightest of pats on Sophia's hand.

Sophia pretended not to notice the brief touch, but Luke didn't miss the hint of a smile that crossed her lips before she spoke again. "Herbie, you should have dinner with us."

"Well, I don't know that Sharla—"

"Sharla will love having someone to talk to besides me." Sophia whirled about to face Luke. "What about you? How are your tablemates?"

"I, uh, don't have any."

Sophia frowned. "Why not?"

"Well…" *My boss pulled a fast one* didn't seem like the right answer. "It just worked out that way."

"Then it's settled. I'll notify the maître d' that we want a table for four." Sophia turned to the crew member walking up to the piano.

Luke and Herbie looked at each other, neither one ready to do battle with Sophia. Herbie shrugged first, and then Luke laughed to himself. If nothing else, he'd be willing to take bets that dinner for the rest of the cruise would prove to be quite entertaining. Besides, it would give him the opportunity to learn more about the woman who had made herself at home in the back of his mind.

"I swear some people are so oblivious." Sharla slid into the chair between him and Sophia. "I kept telling Lydia that I needed to catch up to you, but she'd have none of that until I heard all about her nephew."

"Bad enough the woman talked so much that we almost had to skip dessert to make it here on time. Which one of her kin is he?" Sophia asked, her forehead once again creased in thought.

"The one in New Jersey. Her sister Delilah's boy. Forty-two, never married."

"What does this nephew do?" Sophia asked.

"He's a corrections officer."

Sophia's face lost all expression. The fire in her eyes turned to ice. "Oh."

"Besides"—Sharla sported the same cold expression, only her eyes held something more akin to pain—"I'm guessing *single at forty-two* means he has a boyfriend who he hasn't introduced to his aunt Lydia yet."

Sophia hitched a shoulder in a casual shrug.

Luke cast a sideways glance in Herbie's direction. He'd caught the women's strong reaction to the nephew's job also. But Luke suspected Herbie didn't know what to make of it any more than he did. All he knew was he very much wanted to take away Sharla's pain.

The volume on the PA system shot unexpectedly high, blaring some unrecognizable tune with a lot of electric guitar. The crew guy playing with the equipment threw a cheeky grin over his shoulder. "Sorry about that, Ladies and Gentlemen. But now that I have your attention…" He continued to explain the rules of the game. Essentially they were playing *Name That Tune*. The crew staff guy would play the beginning notes of a popular eighties' tune twice before moving on.

Sophia leaned forward in her seat, whispering the same sacred info about no talking and protecting the answer sheet that had applied during the afternoon trivia game.

Sharla walked up to the piano for their score sheets and pencils.

Earlier in the day Luke hadn't noticed the way she walked. Her hips had just the right amount of swoosh to them. Not enough to advertise, but just enough to entice. And he was definitely enticed. And then some.

Ready for the game to start, everyone waited for the first tune, except Herbie. His gaze was on the crowds moving along the hall outside the lounge.

Luke didn't have to ask why. Apparently he wasn't the only one interested in George and Gloria Bailey.

The lone empty chair at the table had been between her grandmother and Luke. Sharla didn't like the way her senses came alive whenever he was near. Until now she hadn't had to deal with the path her life had taken. She still missed Danny, but the acrid ache that had made itself at home—from the minute her husband's partner had showed up on her doorstep that miserable Thursday night—had dulled to a tepid twinge so vague that sometimes she'd actually forget it was there.

But not until she'd hugged Luke had she wanted to do something about the emptiness that had settled in beside the hurt. And that had her shaking in her sandals. It was one thing for her head to tell her it was time to move on. To find someone new. To start living. But it was another to act on it. Especially with such a handsome man who probably wanted nothing more from her than a vacation fling.

"Ooh. I know that one." Her grandmother scribbled "Kokomo" by The Beach Boys on the first line.

Luke agreed and smiled at Nana, and Sharla felt her

stomach clench. Sexy *and* nice. *Oh, brother*, what was she going to do about this guy? She'd never been the have-a-fling sort of girl. Not in school. Not when she'd moved out on her own. And certainly not now. So, where did that leave her?

Luke scribbled "Don't Worry, Be Happy" on a piece of paper, and, for a short second, she actually wondered if he could read her mind. Then when Nana copied the name onto the answer sheet, Sharla realized that was the name of song number two. *Get a grip.*

Five tunes later, she finally recognized a song, and, pulling away the scratch paper from Luke, her hand brushed against his, and her stomach did that little rolling-surge thing that almost had her forgetting Whitney Houston's "I Wanna Dance with Somebody." When Luke smiled up at her, she came too close to forgetting everything, including that she didn't do flings.

By the time the few notes were played for the last song, she'd pretty much decided the best thing she could do was lock herself in her room for the rest of the cruise, toss out all her books by her favorite romance authors and catch up on nothing but hard-boiled mysteries. Preferably with lots of dead bodies.

Since she and Luke were just little kids for most of the eighties, and Nana and Herbie were not likely to have been listening to the radio either, their team was missing five of the twenty song titles. Nana and Luke were meant for each other when it came to a competitive streak. The two listened intently as the crew member, Jose from Costa Rica, quickly ran through the songs one last time. At number sixteen Luke snapped his fingers, scribbled "Maneater" directly on the answer sheet, and Sharla could feel the heat rising up her neck and filling her cheeks.

Thankfully she was pretty sure no one noticed. Papers were exchanged, and Jose asked for the title of the first song. Just about everyone in the lounge shouted "Kokomo," and, when Jose played the tune the crowd continued singing about Aruba and Jamaica. With every song the room got louder, and people sang longer. Everyone smiling and laughing.

Except for Herbie. During the game he hadn't made a single suggestion. From time to time he'd look at Nana and smile to himself. Usually when Nana guessed at a song and either Sharla or Luke had confirmed Nana's guess. But for most of the time Herbie seemed to be more interested in people watching. A few times Sharla wondered if he had been looking for someone in particular, but, now that the game was over, his attention was all on her grandmother.

Sharla wasn't sure what she thought of that yet either. What she really needed was some air and a little distance from Luke "Brooklyn" Chapman to get her head on straight. "If you'll excuse me, I think I'll take a little walk outside."

"Sounds like a great idea." Luke stood. "If you don't mind, I'd like to join you."

Join her?

Three pairs of eyes settled on her, and all she could manage to mutter was "Sure."

"Don't forget." Nana smiled. "The Gender Game is at ten."

"Gender Game?" Luke and Herbie echoed slowly.

Nana's smile spread a little wider. "In the Windward Lounge, one deck down."

Herbie flipped his wrist to check the time, then extended his arm to Nana. "It's after nine. Shall we go save seats?"

"Great minds think alike." Nana slid her hand around his elbow, and Sharla would have sworn her grandmother looked ten years younger.

"I don't know what to make of that," she said aloud to her grandmother's back disappearing down the corridor.

"Sophia and Herbie?"

She nodded. Something told her that, by the time tonight was over, she was going to need a lot more than a little fresh air.

CHAPTER EIGHT

"Have you used the track on the upper deck yet?" Luke asked.

Sharla pulled her attention away from her grandmother's retreating form. "No, I haven't."

The older couple strolled on, laughing and leaning against each other. They were cute. But he got the feeling Sharla didn't see it that way. "If the wind's not too bad, the track is a nice place for a stroll."

Waiting for the elevator, they stood in silence. Once or twice Sharla glanced in his direction and offered a polite smile. Tight, almost nervous.

When the doors opened, the people in the already crowded space pressed back to make room for them. A little boy about waist high, staring at the floor, turned and looked up at his mother. "Who changes the floor?"

"Who what?" she asked.

The kid pointed to the letters on the carpet. "Yesterday it said Thursday. Now it says Friday. Who changes that?"

All eyes in the elevator dropped to read the day in the middle of the floor.

"I don't know, sweetie." Mom returned her gaze to the panel of escalating numbers.

"Can I stay up and watch?"

"Watch what?"

"When the day changes."

Oh, this kid had the exasperated-with-his-parents eye roll down pat. He was going to be one heck of a teenager.

Without glancing away from her focus on the elevator's progress, the mother shook her head. "No, Brandon. That's past your bedtime."

Brandon stared at the floor until the elevator reached the next stop. Everyone shifted to let some passengers off and other passengers on. Brandon continued to stare at the floor even with the repositioning of people in the confined glass box. The next *ding* announced the arrival to the pool deck. Brandon's mom took hold of his hand, and the two walked into the hallway, the kid's neck craned to keep an eye on the elevator floor.

The doors slid shut, the elevator bounced upward, and Luke leaned against Sharla. "Bet you ten to one, if we ride this elevator at midnight tonight, little Brandon will be here too, waiting to unleash the magic of the changing days."

Just then the elevator opened one floor up on the top deck, and Sharla let out a muffled chuckle. "I don't take a sucker's bet."

He resisted the urge to give her the slightest peck on her cheek. Instead he lifted his shoulder and flashed her that I-gave-it-my-best-shot smile that could usually melt the ice around any woman's heart. When Sharla did a double step, almost tripping off the elevator, his pride hoped his smile had the same effect on her that she was having on him.

The jogging path consisted of a yellow swath painted on the deck in a figure eight overlooking the pool area the next deck down. Restless last night, he'd scoped out the ship and the deck, and had decided his morning run would be more productive in the gym than out here. Especially faced with the risk of running over some well-meaning granny out for her morning constitution. "Three times around is a mile. You up for it?"

"As long as this isn't a race, I'm up for it."

He glanced down at her feet. No flimsy flip-flops or fancy sandals. Practical loafers. Then his gaze traveled up slim ankles to well-shaped calves, and he dragged his focus back to her face before she hauled off and hit him for checking her out that way. "Agreed. No racing."

A few feet onto the path her shoulders relaxed, and he heard her suck in a deep breath and slowly release it, followed by the tiniest hint of a sincere smile. "I would have thought the wind would be stronger."

"It will be when we turn around the bow."

"Bow?"

"Forward part of the ship. The wind is so mild tonight, it probably won't be any stronger than riding in the front seat of a convertible."

"I love the feel of the wind on my face." Sharla tipped her chin upward.

The moonlight shone on her face so he could see every dip and contour, and Luke almost swallowed his tongue. Good grief, she was beautiful.

"My husband had a motorcycle. An old Honda 750. Whenever we could, we'd steal away for a few hours and just ride."

Something inside him tightened up at the word *husband*. He'd already assumed from the rings on her right hand that there had to have been a husband at some time, but he didn't think she was still married. At least he'd hoped not. And yet the far-off look in her eyes, someplace happy, made him wish she were still that happy, even if it meant being married to another man. "You don't ride anymore?"

The light in her eyes vanished as quickly as it had appeared. She shook her head. "No. Not anymore."

Her pace seemed to slow as they came across the first turn around the bow, and he found himself overwhelmed with the need to reach out and fold her hand in his.

"This really is nice." The tension in her stance slipped away. "The air is so fresh and the sound of the waves lapping against the boat so calming."

"It can get in your blood if you're not careful."

"Cruising?"

"Sailing of any kind."

"You sail often?"

This time he shook his head and, in a very unmilitarylike manner, shoved his hands in his pockets to avoid reaching over and grabbing her hand. "Not anymore. But this is my first pleasure cruise."

"And you're alone?"

He bobbed his head. "Do you and your grandmother

cruise a lot?"

"Heavens, no." They circled around the edge. The wind blew at their backs, and she fought a futile battle, fingering her hair away from her eyes. "I wouldn't even be here now if my cousin hadn't had an emergency C-section. Nana was supposed to sail with my great-aunt Leticia. Instead she's with her daughter. Leticia was the youngest of the sisters and had my cousin Nelda rather late in life for her generation. In contrast, not so unusual for today, my cousin is having her first child at thirty-eight."

"How's she doing?"

"Mother and child are fine. But Great-Aunt Leticia didn't want to leave. Her first and possibly only grandchild, and all that."

"So you stepped in."

"I did."

"And what does your husband say about that?" The way her grin slipped and her gaze fell, he wished he could take back the words.

"Danny died three years ago."

"I'm sorry for your loss." He'd said that too many times in the line of duty. So many wives, husbands, mothers, fathers, children left behind. And the words could do so little. "His health or an accident?"

"Murder."

Luke almost lost his footing.

"Danny was a policeman. Vice squad. Wrong place, wrong time."

How many times could he and any other military man say the same? Again, too many. Now he understood the bitter reactions at the mention of a corrections officer. Another potentially dangerous job. He searched for new words. Some way to make it better. To wipe away the hurt. Pushing aside the time-worn platitudes, all he was left with was the need to pull her into his arms and protect her from any more pain. Not an option. Yet.

"We had three good years. You hear of wives always worrying about their husbands not coming home. That, when he walks out the door, you might not see him again. I was convinced I didn't have to." The tautness in her face gave way to a strained smile. "I told him I loved him when he left that morning. At least I'd done that much. Some people's last words aren't kind. I was lucky."

They'd made a third turn around, and, when she kept walking, so did he.

"What about you?" She briefly turned toward him, her smile a bit more genuine, less forced.

"Never married." Odds of success were worse than low in his line of work.

"Tempted?"

"To tie the knot?" He chuckled. "No."

"Ah. A staunch bachelor."

"Absolutely." Even though his work these last two years hadn't allowed for much time to keep company with the ladies, under normal circumstances he enjoyed women. Especially those with feminine curves.

"Workaholic too?"

"That's what my boss says. Which is why I'm here. Two years' accumulated vacation time." Mentioning the near loss of his life in the mother of all shoot-outs, culminating in a hand-to-hand tumble with the last terrorist on his hit list, would not, under the circumstances, be well received.

"Me too. Use them or lose them. My boss wouldn't even consider letting me lose them, so here I am. Well, I had planned to spend it at home catching up on my to-do list and my to-be-read pile, but you've already heard the part about Great-Aunt Leticia." Again she looked up at him. "I get the no-wife thing, but why are you here alone? Surely there's a girl somewhere?"

"No." Thanks to his recent stint fighting bad guys, his proverbial little black book was pathetically out of date. "What about a pretty girl like you? You must have men standing in line to court you."

"*Court me.* Very old-fashioned words from such a modern man."

"I'm a very old-fashioned bachelor."

"Which is probably why you're still a bachelor. I can

see it now. You're going to be another Warren Beatty. Turn forty and realize all you've missed in life. Marry a beautiful woman and crank out five beautiful children and live a beautiful—and charmed—life."

"Beautiful *and* charmed?" He loved how easily she made him laugh. Simple, honest, no ulterior motives, no games. "So who will your Prince Charming be?"

"Oh, that's easy. An ordinary man. Someone with a nine-to-five job. No doctors. No late-night emergency calls. No missing soccer games for patients."

"Sounds like the voice of experience."

She nodded. "I'm an ER nurse at County Medical. The only women who want to marry doctors have never worked with them."

"Got it. No doctors."

"And no heroes. No firemen or policemen. And absolutely no soldiers. If I ever have another relationship, it is going to be as normal as can be."

"Right up to the dog and two-point-five children?"

"*Abso-lute-ly*," she emphasized.

And wasn't that the shame of it. He'd been around the block enough times to recognize which women would be fun, which would be trouble, and which were off-limits. Everything about Sharla shouted home and hearth. Her dedication to her grandmother was proof enough his instincts were right. She was definitely something special. But if he'd harbored even the slightest inkling to test the waters, she'd just slammed the hatch shut on him.

Navy SEAL was most likely high on her Do-Not-Associate-With list. CIA undercover agent would be number one, and flagged in red with skulls and crossbones doodled all around. Which was fine, since he wasn't looking for a relationship. All he had wanted from this vacation was a little fun. And Sharla wasn't the sort for a tryst. No matter what, she would have to remain "hands off". Even if everything about her felt like coming home.

CHAPTER NINE

At almost ten o'clock the Windward Lounge was packed.

Luke scanned the front of the room for Sophia and Herbie. Sure enough, front row, center court, Sophia sat sipping a tall drink with a fruit slice perched on the rim but no sign of Herbie. Just as Luke was about to mindlessly set his hand around the small of Sharla's back to direct her toward her grandmother, she nudged him gently with her elbow, pointed to the front and maneuvered her way through the crowded lounge.

Sophia promptly introduced Luke and Sharla to the passengers at either table beside them.

The woman had been busy. "Where's Herbie?" he asked.

Jutting out her chin as though just noticing he wasn't here, Sophia frowned. "He went to the men's room, but that was a while ago." Her mouth briefly twisted to one side, and then her expression eased back into a smile. "I bet he took a detour by the slots. He loves those nickel machines."

The Gender Game wasn't set to start for fifteen more minutes. Luke took in another fast survey of the room and decided he had time to make a quick run to the casino to check on Herbie. Not that the older man could get himself into very much trouble playing nickel slots, but Luke's gut was rumbling, and he'd learned long ago never to disregard his gut when it chose to speak up. "I'll be right back."

Already engrossed in conversation with the two couples to their left, Sharla merely nodded, but Sophia shot him an impish grin. "Go get him, tiger."

"Aye, aye, captain." With a casual salute, Luke did a

military spin and, keeping a lookout for Herbie, headed for the casino.

As Sophia had predicted, Herbie was in the casino but not playing the slots. More like hiding behind them. It only took a few seconds for Luke to see why. Herbie was watching George at the bar with another man. Being too far away to hear what was said, Luke was sure Herbie most likely could. Every so often Herbie would scribble something on a small spiral notepad that fit in his breast pocket.

Sliding behind a slot machine himself, Luke watched Herbie watching George talking up the guy beside him. When the two men finally separated, Herbie stood and, rather than follow George, followed the man George had been talking with to the Leeward Lounge.

Having settled in a dark corner, continuing to watch Herbie and his target, Luke would have been more entertained watching paint dry. Not much seemed to be happening. Until the wife of the man under surveillance joined him. A waiter took the couple's order, and, at the same moment when the waiter had reached the bar, Herbie sidled up beside him and handed the bartender an empty glass. While the waiter and barman were busy behind the counter, Herbie slipped his hand over the keycard still resting on the round tray, flipped his palm to read the card, then returned it and pulled out the notebook from his pocket. When the bartender handed him a replenished drink, he smiled, uttering what was most likely a thank-you, slipped him a bill and walked away.

At the elevator banks Luke caught up with Herbie on his way to rendezvous with Sophia. "Hey."

Startled out of his thoughts, Herbie glanced over his shoulder at Luke. "Oh, hi. Just going to meet the girls."

Luke didn't have to look at his watch. He knew what time it was. The game would probably be almost over by the time they got there. "Same here."

Herbie patted his breast pocket, as though nervous his notes might be gone, and then waited without a word for the elevator to stop on the Gender Game floor.

Inside the spacious lounge Luke directed Herbie to Sophia's table, except Sophia wasn't there. Neither was Sharla. After too many years fighting bad guys in ugly places, Luke's instincts set him on high alert before his eyes caught sight of grandmother and granddaughter on stage. Each holding a big cardboard number in front of them and running in circles around four other women.

On the other side of the stage, six men did the same thing, but the women came to a stop first. From left to right they displayed the number the game host had been repeating over the loud speaker: 164,532. The women won the point.

Next came the ship's rendition of a human phone booth. Each group stood locked in a wide-armed circle while as many same-gender passengers crammed inside the circle. The ladies were the first to realize that raising their arms in the air allowed for more people to fit. In the end the women were ahead three to two and crowned the Better Gender. At least for tonight.

Luke had to admit it had been a long while since he'd smiled and laughed as much as he had in the last few hours in the company of Sharla and her grandmother. Though when he looked at Sharla, laughing was the last thing he felt like doing. The need to reach out and hold her came fast and hard and often. Never could he remember wanting the simplest of connections more than he wanted air to breathe. Pure unadulterated lust he was used to. He was a sailor after all. Nothing unusual about a girl in every port. But his need to just be near Sharla was totally different. Totally new. And totally terrifying—and not much terrified a SEAL.

"Celebratory drinks are on me." Sophia held up her near-empty glass. "I highly recommend this coconut chi chi. Delicious."

"Just to show I'm a good sport"—Herbie smiled at Sophia—"first round is on me."

"Not me, you two. It's been a long day. All I want is to crawl into bed with my book."

Visions of Sharla crawling into bed were the last thing Luke needed. What he really needed was to get on a computer to see what he could dig up on George and now

Herbie. Maybe that would keep out of his thoughts. *Right.* And the Queen of England drinks bourbon not tea.

"I actually have some work to do." Luke pushed to his feet and turned to Sharla. "I'll walk you back."

"That won't be necessary."

"I didn't say it was."

Sharla frowned; her grandmother beamed, and Herbie chuckled. "Might as well accept it, dear. You can't take chivalry out of the navy."

"Navy?" Sharla's eyes rounded in surprise at Luke.

"Not anymore." He wasn't going to elaborate. If the words *Central Intelligence Agency* came out of his mouth, she'd never let him walk her to her cabin, and, though he had no intention of acting on his attraction to her, he very much wanted to escort her safely to her room. "Shall we go?"

Gathering up a light shawl, Sharla stepped out in front of him and walked to the exit. At the elevators she turned to face him. "I don't think there's much risk of being mugged on my way to my cabin."

"Did I say there was?"

"The cabin stewards are all over the place, tending to rooms and doing whatever it is they do."

"Making animals out of folded towels."

That made her face light up. "They are good. I got a puppy dog wearing my sunglasses."

"Monkey hanging from the ceiling."

Her eyes did that rounded thing again. "How'd they do that?"

"With a coat hanger."

"I hope I get one."

"It's a long cruise. I'm sure we're going to see quite a menagerie."

The elevator opened on the fifth floor. She stepped out and came to an abrupt stop when he followed her. "You really don't have to do this."

"I'm heading to the computer stations on the other end of the ship. You're on my way."

He recognized the moment she resigned herself to an

escort. Her breath blew out heavily, and her shoulders relaxed. But the giveaway was the gentle shaking of her head. "You win."

He didn't even try to hold back the smile that took over his face. "I always do."

Each step down the narrow hall made Sharla more intimately aware of the man at her heels. Ignoring him was becoming increasingly difficult. Especially since he seemed intent on inserting himself in her path at every turn. Which, considering they appeared to be one of the few single adults on the ship under the age of sixty, shouldn't come as a surprise to her. She just wished he wasn't so… much.

At her room, she slid in the keycard, dipped the handle and shoving open the heavy door, turned to glance at him over her shoulder. Determination to hurry inside and keep away from the temptation that was Luke Chapman waged a small war with the sappy girl who wanted to simply stand there and stare at him. Or worse, pull him into her arms and kiss him until they docked in the next port.

Luke bobbed his head and, to her chagrin, took a step back. "I don't think I need to check under the bed for the bogeyman."

Words wouldn't come. Luke's deep hypnotic voice was enough to turn her mouth dry. The best she could do was shake her head, and even then she wanted very much to nod and have him come check under the bed, around the bed, on the bed. Dear heavens, what was she doing to herself?

"Good night."

His voice had dropped an octave, and the raspy sound had her almost regretting her no-flings rule. But learning he'd been a navy man only confirmed her initial impressions and explained the determined-bachelor thing. A girl in every port and all that.

Swallowing hard, she croaked "Good night" and, closing the cabin door behind her, fell heavily against it.

Her heart racing like an overeager thoroughbred. It was definitely time to make a change in her life. Someplace in South Florida there had to be a banker or an insurance salesman with piercing eyes and a voice that could melt butter. And the Queen of England drank coffee not tea.

Way too close for comfort. When Sharla had turned to face him, Luke swore he'd seen the same raw attraction in her eyes that pumped through his veins. He also saw vulnerability and confusion and an emotion that had him taking a step back—fear.

His every nerve ending was still hyperaware of her. She might as well be standing next to him and not in her cabin down the hall. Even though it had been hours since the casual hug, there was no shaking the feel of her. Walking past one of the many cocktail lounges, he was tempted to grab a beer to take off some of the edge, but he knew he'd need a lot more than a few drinks to get Sharla out of his system.

Time to focus. Taking the stairs to the next deck up, Luke ran through the back of his mind what he'd observed today of Herbie and George, not allowing himself to think of Sharla. Finding an isolated cubicle in the far corner, and ignoring the grossly overpriced minutes, he logged onto the ship's Internet. Five very long minutes later he was barely able to maneuver his way through the slow-moving cyberworld in search of a middle-aged George Bailey.

This was insane. Going a different route, he typed in a personal message address for Kate, the tech genius at his office, and wrote *Hi, beautiful*. Within seconds, a box popped up in the corner of his screen.

KATE: *Back at ya, handsome. This is a surprise.*

Any past interaction between him and Kate had always happened on The Company's accounts. Since this was neither business, nor did he want his boss to discover he was not totally resting, he approached Kate on her personal account. Besides, if anything came of his inquiries, it would be best if none of this were traceable through official channels.

LUKE: On the high seas as ordered. I need a favor. Her lack of response lasted a bit too long, then the little stars that showed her typing finally appeared.

KATE: If I lose my job, you get to supplement my unemployment.

LUKE: Absolutely! He didn't need to worry about that. Techno geeks with the skill set of Kate—and honest to boot—were not that easy to find. The Company would turn many a blind eye before letting her go.

KATE: Liar. Whatcha need?

Steadily he gave her all the info, what little there was, on George.

KATE: I may be good, Bigboy, but I'm not that good. I need something else. A birth date, hometown, high school. Even narrowing it down to men over forty and under seventy with wives named Gloria, and assuming he was born somewhere in New England because he's a Red Sox and Bruins fan, I've still got triple-digit possibilities.

LUKE: What about Herbert Klein? Former Philadelphia policeman, retired. Former Marine, probably around—Before he could finish typing, a new pop-up box sprang open.

KATE: Wow. Two silver stars, a Purple Heart, commendations for valor. The list goes on. He should have his own TV show.

That made Luke laugh. He could picture it now, Herbie and a couple of old war cronies in plaid shorts, white socks and sandals, setting up shop as PIs, chasing bad guys for sixty minutes every Thursday night at eight o'clock.

LUKE: I'm looking for something out of the ordinary and recent.

KATE: Nada. This guy makes squeaky clean look dirty. Wife Marjorie passed away thirty years ago. No children. Never remarried. Shares a condo with his brother-in-law, also a widower. Volunteers for Habitat for Humanity and a local soup kitchen.

So why the heck is he following George?

LUKE: Keep poking around, please. I'll check in tomorrow night to see if you found anything.

KATE: Will do, and don't break too many hearts.

He knew she was grinning at him. Kate had worked IT at The Company for eons before he'd arrived. She was over forty and dressed like a college coed on the make. He had no idea if she was married or single, had kids of the two or four-legged variety or how the heck she managed to find obscure data in the blink of an eye, but she always came through.

KATE: Got something. May not mean anything but, around six months ago, his brother-in-law moved some serious change around and then nada.

LUKE: How serious?

KATE: Almost all he had. Fifty thousand.

Luke whistled. Still had no idea how she accessed information like that so fast, but, if she were here, he'd get down on bended knee and kiss her feet.

LUKE: You're still my only girl. Keep working on Bailey.

KATE: Slave driver. ☺

Cringing at the amount of time he'd spent logged on to the ship's computer, he signed off and decided to see if Mr. Bailey was still out and about. Keeping an eye on the guy would be easier on Luke than going back to his cabin to crawl into bed alone, stare at the ceiling and think of Sharla. Nope. R & R was overrated. Time to track down one George and Gloria Bailey.

CHAPTER TEN

When the hell had he grown so much older? Luke rolled over and climbed out of bed at… 9:00 a.m. It was a SEAL's standard to be fit, to be at the ready anytime, anywhere. The last two years under deep cover had kept him from partying all night, but who knew at only thirty-four that a bunch of ladies in red-hats could wear him out?

Especially the one in the wide-brim hat with an hourglass figure. The woman laughed from deep down in her gut, and her smiles always shone in her eyes. They'd done one shot after another, sang along with the piano man—who could most likely outplay Billy Joel—and, when the group of partying females finally called it a night at four in the morning, his sides hurt from laughing; his head hummed from too much booze; and Sharla was still the only woman on his mind.

Splashing cool water on his face now, he rubbed the sleep from his eyes and then dared to look into the mirror. His hair sticking out every which way, and his eyes bloodshot with dark circles underneath, he'd scare his own mother. He had a little less than an hour before meeting Sharla and the gang for morning trivia. If he could manage a fast shower and shave without his head rolling off his shoulders, he could slip in a couple of cups of java before having to face the world.

Three cups of coffee and a plate of scrambled eggs with bacon later, Luke felt almost human. If he wanted to keep going with an early morning fitness routine—so he could return to work when his thirty days were up—there would have to be no more partying with the red-hat ladies. Just to further clear his head, he'd make sure to hit the gym after trivia and make up for the morning workout he'd skipped.

"Good morning, sunshine." Sophia patted the seat next to her.

Sharla looked up from her electronic reader, raised her lips in a quick smile before returning her attention to her book, and Luke felt his breath clog. She had no right to be so blasted attractive in a baggy cover-up, a ponytail and no makeup. He had it bad. And somehow he was going to have to get over it. He was not a permanent kind of guy, and Sharla had *commitment required* oozing from every pore.

Besides, even if he were looking for that special someone to come home to after a mission, Sharla had already determined his career path was not acceptable. All he had to do was remind himself of that whenever the urge crept up to pull her into his arms. Of course the smarter thing to do would be to simply walk away before he got to know her any better and before she worked her way deeper under his skin. But today he wasn't in the mood to be smart.

"All ready for the trivia this morning?" he asked.

"Always." Sophia flashed a sly smile that suddenly shifted wide and bright.

Luke didn't have to turn around to know that Herbie had to be approaching.

Rather than sit across from Sophia in the vacant seat, Herbie pulled over a stool and sat beside her. "Morning, ladies."

Sophia's eyes sparked at the gesture, and Luke bit back a smile of his own. It was nice to know someday, when he was ready, there would still be a nice old gal willing to take on his dowdy old self. Plaid shorts and all. Luke cleared his throat to remind Herbie of his presence.

"And gentleman," Herbie added.

"Done." Sharla slid her e-reader into the fabric pouch beside her. "Sorry about that. I only had the epilogue left, and I really didn't want to wait to finish."

"My late wife always had her nose in a book. The stack of paperbacks by the bed often multiplied into two or three piles." His gaze dropped, and, when he glanced back up, sadness lingered. "She read through almost every last one in the end."

Sophia's small hand slipped over his and squeezed.

When the moment passed, Luke noticed Sophia hadn't let go. By the time the trivia game was ready to start, Herbie had woven his fingers with hers.

When Sharla returned with the multiple pencils and sheets of papers, the older couple's hands were still linked together. The frown that dipped to the bridge of her nose was brief, but he'd caught it. From everything Kate had said last night about Herbie Klein, Sharla didn't have a thing to worry about. The guy was as stand-up as they came.

This morning's trivia went much like yesterday afternoon's. There was only one question which nobody had any idea about. *What is the traditional five-year-anniversary gift?*

Answer sheets had already been exchanged among the teams with one answer left to check, when Gloria came sauntering into the lounge area and practically slithered into the empty chair. "Am I very late?"

Sharla coughed. Sophia blinked. Herbie scowled, and Luke wondered if Gloria's grasp of time was any better for her masseuse and stylist appointments.

"Last answer to the last question," Jose, on the crew staff, announced. "What is the traditional fifth anniversary present?"

"Wood," Gloria answered in chorus with Jose, oblivious to the daggers Sophia's glare cast in her direction.

Luke was surprised the time challenged woman knew anything aside from the diamond and platinum anniversaries.

As the pages were returned to the rightful teams, George strode over and pulled up a stool beside Herbie.

"Glad you could join us." The sarcasm in Gloria's voice belied the sweet expression, though Luke was more intrigued at the implication that she'd been waiting for more than thirty seconds.

"Business is business, dear."

Herbie stiffened in his seat, and Luke wished Kate had

been able to provide more information on Mr. George Bailey.

As Sophia sprang up to collect her prize for seventeen correct responses, Luke turned to George. "What business are you in?"

"Real estate." George leaned forward and lowered his voice. "Smartest move I ever made. Glory and I are set for life." With that, George sat back and waited.

But not for long, as Sophia stood over them, handing out the game-winning prizes: highlighters.

Herbie propped his ankle across his knee and, with a *tsk*ing noise, added, "Must be nice. My portfolio barely trickles in."

Gloria asked Sharla about the book she had just finished.

Another surprise since Luke hadn't expected Gloria to be the sort to have a hobby other than shopping. While Sophia interjected a comment here or there, Luke could tell her attention weighed more heavily on the conversation between Herbie and George.

"So your current investment isn't your first resort to buy into?" Herbie asked.

George puffed up and shook his head. "No. First time I invested in a start-up resort was about five years ago. Turks and Caicos. Beautiful spot. Glory and I were staying at the same hotel as the land developer. I barely got in on the bottom floor of that one."

"Very fortuitous." Luke studied George. If the guy was blowing smoke, he'd had a lot of practice. Didn't flinch at the potentially double-edged comment. Could probably pass a lie detector if Luke had one handy.

"So you've invested in more than one?" Herbie signaled for the waiter. "What'll you have?" he asked George, clearly planning to keep him talking.

"Thanks, scotch."

Herbie looked to Luke.

"Make mine a Bud." No way was he touching the hard stuff at this hour of the day. And didn't that make him feel old. What was happening to him? Couldn't keep up with a bunch of old ladies, couldn't crawl out of bed bright and early, couldn't get one blonde beauty out of his mind and now couldn't handle a real drink at eleven in the morning.

Herbie leaned back again. "You were saying."

"Next time around," George continued, "we got in earlier and had a bigger piece of the deal. So much undeveloped land in Fiji. More and more people are wanting that exclusive escape vacation, and Fiji has everything to offer."

That was one thing George had right. A few years back, after his first mission with Nick Harper's EOD team, Luke and the boys had a chance for some R & R in French Polynesia.

"You been?" George asked Luke. "You've got an awfully big grin on your face."

Herbie dropped his feet to the floor. "He's probably thinking of a woman."

"Probably," Luke added softly, casting a quick glimpse at Sharla to see if she was listening.

She and Gloria were deep in a discussion on the merits of romantic comedy in fiction versus on-screen.

Sophia was still only half listening to the ladies.

He simply didn't know what to make of her.

"Hey, handsome."

A familiar feminine voice came from behind Luke that caught Sharla's notice.

Luke pushed to his feet and turned to last night's singing group. "Morning, ladies."

Ms. Wide-Brimmed Red Hat stopped in front of him. "Did you get enough sleep?"

He could feel everyone's gazes burning into his back. There was no need to turn around. The sudden pause in the book discussion told him that he and Red Hat Lady had Sharla's full attention.

"Yes, thanks. And you?"

"For sure. But I'm the one who should be thanking you. You were such a good sport taking up with an old woman like me."

Silence lingered like an awkward waiter.

"Me too," a shorter woman with gray hair chimed in. "The old goats on this boat are no fun, and they sure as heck couldn't have kept up with the three of us the way you did."

Someone at the table gasped, and he realized he needed to clarify the conversation for their audience. "I'm sorry to admit my vocal skills are seriously lacking, but anytime you ladies want to close down the piano bar again, just let me know."

And, with that bit of explanation, the conversations behind him resumed. One bullet dodged.

"I don't suppose you play whist?" Red Hat Lady asked.

"Sorry, ma'am." He shook his head. "My mama never got past teaching me poker."

"Now there's an idea."

Her eyes twinkled with mischief, and, not for the first time, Luke gave the woman a mental pat on the back. Way to grow older with grace and fun.

"We'd better sit before the rest of the girls get here and take the good seats."

For just a second Luke wondered if older women ever stopped thinking of themselves as girls. He certainly hoped not.

Why did Sharla want to show her claws and scratch out the red-hat woman's eyes? Sharla had no claim on Luke, and, by the end of the conversation, she realized neither did the woman who had to be at least fifteen years older than she looked. But that didn't change the way Sharla felt.

Forcing her attention away from Luke, and who did or didn't flirt with him, she caught a glimpse of Nana scoping out Gloria's husband. And now here Sharla sat, only half listening to Gloria as Sharla checked out her grandmother only half listening to them while checking out the men's conversation. *What in the name of all that was holy was happening to her?*

For the first time in years, Sharla had not only noticed a

man but she was having one heck of a hard time resisting him. And now she was doing her best to look at the other men as potential marks, wondering what her grandmother found so interesting.

Maybe all Sharla needed was to get off the dumb ship for some fresh air and a new perspective. Or maybe she needed to watch her grandmother like a hawk before they all wound up in the slammer.

CHAPTER ELEVEN

After the group-rousing interruption from Red Hat Lady, the conversation never returned to real estate. And later that afternoon, Gloria showed up solo for trivia. She explained that her husband was on a conference call.

Roaming rates on a cell phone from out in the middle of the ocean were not cheap, and reception was often iffy even in the biggest cities. That left Luke chewing on doubts about if this guy was legit or putting on a great show. Or, more likely, scouting for a better pigeon than Herbie.

But it was Sharla's absence from the team that took up most of Luke's thoughts. Not wanting to look anxious, he was delighted when Gloria quickly asked if Sharla would be joining them. Already in Trivia Queen mode, Sophia offhandedly made a comment about *hooked on a new book and soaking up the sun* before she settled into her routine for another round of high-stakes cruise ship trivia.

Winning again—not surprisingly—they were awarded the coveted cruise ship calendars… that expired in six months. So far Luke had amassed an impressive collection of ship brand junk.

Now he found himself primping at the mirror like a pimply faced teen hoping to score a date with the head cheerleader. How big a fool was he really?

Tossing down the comb, he ignored the impulse to take one last look and walked out the cabin door. Tonight would be his first night having dinner with Sophia and Sharla in the three-story dining room. And, as luck would have it, tonight was also the first formal dining night.

When Conway had insisted Luke pack a tux, he'd come

close to laughing in his boss' face. But a man didn't spend eleven years in Uncle Sam's Navy without getting used to wearing monkey suits. Though deep inside Luke wished he wore dress whites instead of the black tux.

Not that it mattered, but he'd yet to meet a lady who could resist a man in a dress uniform. Across the dining room he spotted his new table. Or more accurately he spotted Sharla. The red dress had a sheen to it, something like satin. Thin straps formed a square neckline that showed just enough cleavage to whet a man's appetite and have him dreaming of possibilities. Not that it mattered.

Taking a sip as she glanced up from the table, Sharla almost breathed in her water. Wow, that man knew how to wear a tuxedo. "Herbie and Nana stopped to have their photos taken. They should be here any second." Not that he'd asked, but she needed to say something besides *hot, hot, hot*.

He pulled out the seat beside her. "You look lovely."

"Thank you. You look pretty good yourself."

"You think?" One side of his mouth lifted in that know-it-all smile that made her stomach do strange things.

Rather than respond to his question, she buried her nose in the single-page menu. "The waiter recommends the chilled watermelon soup this evening."

"Anything else?"

"Mmm. Rack of lamb and lemon meringue tart."

He bobbed his head but kept his eyes on the menu.

The quiet lingered, and, when she'd finally made up her mind and set aside her menu, her gaze collided with his.

"Did you enjoy the book?"

She nodded. "Several of the books in my to-be-read pile are from my favorite authors. I've been anxious to start this one. It's the first of a new series." That answer was a lot easier to produce than *she didn't have the strength to sit across from him at trivia and talk herself out of hugging the stuffing out of him.*

"Tell me about your job." He brought the glass of water to his lips without ever taking his eyes off her.

"Most of the time I love it. Ever since I volunteered in high school as a candy striper in the emergency room, I knew that's where I wanted to be."

"So you're a trauma nurse."

"Got the battle scars to prove it." She turned her arm to show a two-inch line at the base of her elbow. "A frightened teen didn't want anyone on staff touching him. I got too close."

"Didn't realize you work in a tough neighborhood."

"Not anymore. But this was from my days in Chicago. Before I got the urge to fly south for the winter and never flew back."

"Everything's sunny and bright in the Sunshine State."

She shook her head and stole a quick sip of water. "I've seen things no member of the human race should have to. Kids brought in with half their brains gone after a drive-by shooting. Entire families mangled and broken at the hands of a drunk driver. Women battered, beaten and broken, limping out the door with the men who promise it will never happen again."

A slow blink at her words might have been for things he didn't want to imagine, or perhaps things he'd also seen. She didn't know which. But she wasn't surprised when his hands atop the table curled into fists at the mention of domestic abuse. There was so much more to this man than a pretty face, and she very much wanted to dig around and uncover all the interesting facets of Luke "Brooklyn" Chapman. "Interesting nickname, *Brooklyn*. Do you live in New York?"

His head turned from side to side. "Nope. Live in Virginia now. Got the call sign from the navy. Only guy from New York out of a group of fifty. And even on a good day I still sounded like Joe Pesci in *My Cousin Vinny*."

"What's a *yewt*?" Smiling she repeated the famous line from the popular movie.

Luke dabbed the sides of his mouth with his cloth

napkin, then cleared his throat. "Not for nuttin', but youse guys really know how to berl a good cuppa tea."

"Oh, my God." She had to cover her mouth to stop from drawing attention to her laughter. From behind her hand she mumbled, "You did not really talk that way."

He laughed. "Oh, yes. Hence the nickname."

"But you don't talk like that now."

"Every once in a while a word slips out. Anytime I'm around New Yorkers, I hear myself saying things like *cawfey* and *chawclet* and *shua*."

"*Shua?*"

This time he chuckled. "*Sure.*"

"Oh." She tried not to laugh again. "*Shua.*"

"You two look to be having a good time without us." Sophia stepped toward the seat Herbie pulled out for her. The only table available had been for six, so the four of them sat across from each other leaving the end chairs empty.

"Not possible, Sophia." Luke hurriedly stood, only sitting down again after Sophia was comfortably seated.

"Charmer. You remind me of my late husband. Benny could sweet-talk the shirt off your back, then turn around and sell it to you."

"Nana!"

"Oh, Luke knows that's a compliment. I married your grandfather, didn't I?"

Some days Sharla wondered if she and her grandmother were really blood relations or if perhaps, like in the gypsy fables, she'd been left on a doorstep somewhere and simply raised by a band of do-good grifters.

For the next hour the conversation roamed from Luke growing up the youngest of four kids in a half-Irish, half-Italian household, to Sharla being an only child and loving the times when her archeologist father would let her join him for a project. Not that she was ever allowed near any of the important digs, but just listening to her father's stories at bedtime had fascinated her about what day-to-day life had been like in the world he was unraveling.

Once they were settled in at the Leeward Lounge,

waiting for the Elvis music trivia contest, the stories shifted to Herbie and some of his craziest cases. Though he only shared the more amusing ones, like the burglars who had paused to sign in to their victim's computer to check their own Facebook page and didn't bother to sign out. Or the drunk idiots who drove into the DA's house and fled the scene but left the car registered in their name sticking out of his basement.

Nana had been a true master, always flawlessly redirecting the conversation whenever anyone asked what she and her husband had done in their day.

Now that Sharla thought about it, all of Luke's stories were from when he was growing up. He knew she was a nurse. And she knew he'd been in the navy but had no idea what he did now.

The pretty brunette with the English accent stepped up to the piano bench with paper and pencils, and began warming up the crowd.

With a larger crowd than last night, Sophia had been lucky to find an open table. Since George and Gloria had told them earlier they had reservations for a cozy supper at the Italian specialty restaurant, there'd been no need to procure extra seating. And frankly Sharla was relieved not to have to worry about what Nana was up to with Gloria's husband. Even if Sharla had decided she was simply overreacting. But then again, all she had to do was think to the first day on the ship when Nana had taken a dive for a good seat, and those niggling doubts teased at the back of her mind again. Why couldn't she have been born into a family of nice, boring Iowa corn farmers?

Elvis' popularity through the generations created stiffer competition than the music trivia contest from the night before. Correctly guessing twenty out of twenty tunes, Sophia had to share the winning glory with two other teams. And the key chain prizes.

"Well, if you ladies"—Herbie turned briefly to Luke—"and gent, will excuse me, I'd like to get out of this penguin costume."

"Oh, but you look so handsome." Sophia actually batted her eyes at the man.

"Hopefully I'll be just as handsome in my shorts and sandals. Be right back."

Sophia's gaze remained on Herbie's back. Her smile easy, almost whimsical.

Which meant she either didn't remember that Herbie's room was by the bow or didn't care that the guy was walking toward the stern in the opposite direction of his cabin. Wherever he was going, he was definitely taking the long way around. "I think I'm going to follow the wise man's advice, except I'm going to call it a night." At least Luke hoped this time he'd get to call it a night before morning.

Halfway through the casino he spotted Herbie. Just like last night, he was using the slot machines to hide from George's view.

Only this time George wasn't talking up another man; he was sitting at the blackjack tables, and, judging by the decreasing pile of chips, paying more attention to the comings and goings of other players than to his cards.

Resigned to spending a long while of everyone watching everyone, Luke hadn't expected George to cash in so early.

But rather than follow George to confirm he was turning in for the night, Herbie moved through the crowd to where George had been playing cards.

Setting down his own drink, Herbie counted out a small stack of chips in front of him. He took a sip from his glass, then pulled a handkerchief from his pocket and sneezed into the old-fashioned cloth.

How many men nowadays actually carried handkerchiefs with them? In a move that impressed even Luke, Herbie dumped what had been left of George's drink into his own glass, enfolded the empty one inside the handkerchief and slipped the entombed glass into his jacket pocket. Finally things were getting interesting.

Time for a face to face with Mr. Klein. Luke followed Herbie across the ship and watched as he rode the elevator up to his floor. Sure Herbie had stopped at the right floor for his cabin, Luke took his time climbing the stairs.

Making his way down the narrow halls, he checked the cabin numbers, stopping in front of cabin 1011. Ten and eleven, both his lucky numbers. Had Herbie been in any other room, Luke might not have easily remembered where to find him. Lifting his hand, he gave the door a soft rap.

"Just a minute." Muffled footsteps grew louder. The handle dropped, and the door cracked open halfway. "I won't be needing… Oh, Luke."

He didn't bother waiting for a polite invitation, giving the door a slight nudge as he moved past Herbie. "You don't mind if I join you, do you?"

The quick smile that Herbie had plastered on for Luke's benefit gave way to a curled brow and irritated glare. "Actually—"

"Care to tell me what's really going on?"

"I don't know what you're—"

"Talking about?" Luke pointed to the empty glass on the vanity surrounded by a dark container of eye shadow, a makeup brush and clear tape. "Why do you need George's prints?"

Herbie raked his fingers through his thick salt-and-pepper hair, turned to look at the array of makeshift equipment and, blowing out a deep sigh, pivoted to face Luke again. "You know as well as I do that his name is no more George Bailey than I'm Kris Kringle. There were only two George Baileys born and raised in the Boston area in this crook's age group."

So Luke was right about where Good Old George had come from.

"One died at age ten, probably of an asthma attack, and the other is a retired Marine. This guy's no Marine."

"No, he's not. What's this all about?"

"George Bailey met my brother-in-law, Sid, on a cruise, much like this one. Did a good talk and put on a good show.

Sid is no idiot, so George had to make it work. Took him on a tour of some property on Barbados while they were docked in port."

"Not enough time to research the land."

"Exactly. Sid convinced George to let him in on the deal. Sid's not a rich man, so he had to sell most of his portfolio. You don't get much dividend income from oil and tech stock. The promise of tripling his money in a year when they sold the property to the developer was too much for Sid to ignore."

"I don't get it. He doesn't claim to be the developer."

"No. He's the dealmaker. Sucks his investors into funding a bogus corporation which supposedly buys parcels of land in an as-yet-untouched area. Claims a developer is ready to pay triple for the land with permits etc. ready to build."

"But…"

"The building doesn't happen. Maybe the land is bought, maybe not. Who knows? Bottom line is, there's some problem somewhere, and now they own very expensive shares of nothing."

"That does happen."

Herbie hefted a lazy shrug. "It does. Everyone makes a bad deal once in a while. But why is George still living like Midas?"

"You think he's done this before?"

"And is doing it again. We've tried going through legal channels, but Bailey's office is a dummy address. Vacant. And the phones got disconnected within days of the word going out about how the deal had gone sour. We couldn't find the guy under any rock."

"So how did you find him now?"

A toothy smirk took over Herbie's face. "Let's just say, it pays to have friends in low places."

Luke burst out laughing. Heaven knows he'd spent a boatload of time in low places of late. If Herbie had been a cop in the Northeast for twenty years, he had to have made a connection here and there. From the sound of it, not the kind to list on a job resume.

"I had to make sure it was the same guy."

"And it is?"

"Yeah. I sent my brother-in-law a snapshot. He confirmed."

"So now what?"

"In order to bring down this character, I need to know who I'm dealing with. Find his weak spot."

Luke lifted his chin, pointing in the direction of the glass. "You got someone to send those to?"

"I got a couple of pals still on the force. They'll—"

"I've got better. You any good at this?"

Herbie nodded, his smile still in place.

"Get me a good shot of the prints. I need to make a couple of calls. By morning we'll know exactly who we're dealing with."

CHAPTER TWELVE

L ike a lazy kitty, Sharla stretched her legs and spread her toes. Then she lifted her arms to the ceiling and leaned from side to side. Not as sore as she'd been yesterday morning.

She'd thought she was in good shape. On her feet every day for hours, lifting and turning patients. Pushing around crash carts and other heavy equipment. But working out the last two mornings with Kyle had shown her just how out of shape she was. At least Kyle had been right about one thing. Every day she stuck to it, the morning soreness would lessen.

Her triceps or biceps or whatever they were still stung a bit but not nearly as much as the day before. She was actually looking forward to another workout. Even though she'd been a bit disappointed that she hadn't run into Luke at the fitness center, in the end it had made it easier for her to lift and lunge and not be self-conscious.

"You're up early again." Nana stepped out of the bathroom, dressed and ready to go. Even though she didn't need to catch any worms, she was still an early riser.

"Yeah. I think I'm going to join a gym when we get home. One of those places just for women."

"Or you could join one where you'll meet men."

"Nana." Sharla pushed to her feet and grabbed the towel draped over the desk chair.

"What? You think Danny was the only man out there? You're too young to spend the rest of your life alone. You should find a nice man, settle down—"

"I know, Nana. Have a few children. Someone who will look after me when I'm old."

"That's right." Sophia slipped the day's activity list into its designated slot on her lanyard. "What about Luke? He's a nice boy. Seems to like you too."

"He's a player. He'd like anything in a skirt. You saw him with those women yesterday. The cougar and the tiger. No thank you."

"Things are not always what they seem. He's a good catch. I can tell. He's ready."

"Ready? For what?"

Nana shook her head and patted Sharla on the shoulder. "Good thing you never went into the family business. Your powers of observation are really lousy. Just trust me on this one. Luke Chapman is a man worthy of you. I'm meeting Herbie for breakfast. Want to join us?"

"Nope. Kyle is expecting me in the gym."

"That one's not so bad either. But he's young and still having too much fun. Stick with Luke."

"Nana."

"Meet us upstairs dressed to disembark. By the time trivia's over, most of the folks going ashore will be gone, and we won't have to stand in long lines to get off the ship. And wear the sexy two-piece not the boring blue bathing suit."

"Nana!"

"Sweetie, you'll never catch a man if you don't show your bait."

Last night Luke had sent Kate the photos of the fingerprints. Within minutes data was flowing in fast and heavy. Good Old George was born Antonio Montanaccio in the popular North End of Boston. By the time he was eighteen, he'd had his own revolving door to the Suffolk County Jail. During the day he had worked as a shoe salesman. At night he had done favors for the local crime boss.

At twenty-two he had married Mary DeStefano and had moved to New York. Six months later Antoinette was born.

Followed by Adella and Celeste, and five years in the state pen for breaking and entering. While in Sing Sing, Mary divorced the sorry bum, and, when Antonio was released, "Michael Green" was born. Then came "Ralph King" and "Paul Dempsey," but lady luck had smiled on him when "George Bailey" went into the swindling business.

Kate was gathering what data she could without Conway getting wind of Luke's off-duty curiosities. Luke and Herbie needed to get as much info as possible about the development site in Puerto Rico before they docked in San Juan.

Trivia was still at ten, and Sharla and the gang wanted to hit the ship's beach port in time for the barbecue lunch. Luke, on the other hand, was ready for a little more physical activity. According to the brochures, all sorts of options were available, from renting seaboards to parasailing. But scuba diving had his number. Not many places to dive in the Afghan desert, and, ever since he'd boarded this tin can, the water had been calling his name. Today it would be just him and the fishes.

But first on Luke's agenda was getting his butt to the gym.

"Morning, mate." Kyle the personal trainer waved at Luke.

"Morning."

"Missed ya yesterday."

"Late night."

Kyle's head bobbed. "Yeah, know how that goes. I've got a session starting in five, but let me know if ya need anything."

"Will do. Thanks, man."

Luke stepped off to the side, leaned and turned, stretching his overanxious muscles before getting on the treadmill. Even if catching Bailey wasn't a special op, the thrill of the chase was already building, and it felt better than good.

"Good morning, beautiful." Kyle's voice carried from the reception area. Luke would normally have ignored the voices around him except that he clearly heard a nervous laugh. Sharla's laugh.

Almost missing his step as the treadmill kicked on, Luke began a steady uphill pace, watching the ocean beyond the glass windows, listening for the voices in the exercise room. He'd run less than a mile when being unable to see her got the better of him. Turning off the machine, he shifted places and hopped onto another machine, facing the area where Kyle helped guide Sharla in her workout.

When she leaned back on the exercise ball and elevated her hips, her cutoff T-shirt rising with every lift of her arms to expose the bare skin at her waistline, Luke almost fell face forward into the control panel.

Kyle said something Luke couldn't make out, and she lost her balance, fell on her rear and broke into a fit of laughter. Immediately Kyle reached out to pull her to her feet, and yanked her up off the floor and into his chest. She got flustered. Kyle took a step back, and the adrenaline channeling through Luke's body at the prospect of working a sort-of mission the next few days redirected to his fists and the prospect of knocking Kyle's head off.

For another thirty minutes Luke tortured himself, watching Sharla work out and make smiley faces at the young trainer. "The guy's too young for her."

"Excuse me?" A man near about Luke's age with the beginnings of a beer gut glanced his way.

"Nothing. Just thinking out loud."

"If it's a woman, stop. There's no figuring them out. I've been married for ten years, and trust me. You'll never win."

"Right." Luke looked back at Sharla. He was either going to have to fish or cut bait. And right now, cutting bait wasn't the front-runner.

Showered and changed into the boring blue bathing suit and matching cover-up, Sharla scurried into the lounge to meet up with the trivia team. Gloria was the only one at the table.

"You made it," Gloria said with a bright smile. "How'd the workout go?"

"Great. Except for falling on my butt a time or two."

"Which trainer is working with you?"

"Kyle."

Gloria's brow creased in thought. "The Aussie?"

Sharla nodded.

"Sweet. Young, but sweet."

"Yeah. He makes me laugh, so I don't think about how stupid I look."

"I doubt you look stupid. With your figure, you probably have all the guys in the place drooling."

"Not exactly. Though I do think I make Kyle nervous. Can't quite figure out why."

"Why? Honey, you're Grade A prime."

Sharla resisted the urge to look over her shoulder to see if some svelte woman stood behind her. Not that Sharla was a dog or anything. Danny had fallen all over himself the first time he'd met her. But she was no Marilyn Monroe.

Gloria shrugged. "You going to the beach?"

"Having lunch with Nana, then thought I'd see what I can do in the water. Maybe snorkel."

"Not me." Gloria waved her arm high at Sophia and Herbie coming toward them. "Toes are as far in as I go. Just give me a lounge chair, a piña colada and a cabana boy, and I'm happy."

Now why didn't that surprise Sharla?

The trivia game went about the same as the last few days, except something felt off with Luke. He'd pulled up a stool behind Herbie, even though there was an empty seat next to her. Occasionally he leaned forward to scribble something on a piece of paper for Nana, but not once did he look in her direction until the group broke apart to go ashore. Even then all she got was a casual *see you guys later*. What was with him?

Following her grandmother and Herbie to the elevators, Sharla refused to think about Luke. Next stop—fun in the water.

"Aren't these the best ribs ever?" Sitting at a picnic table under the palms, Sophia groaned over another bite.

"Once on leave, when I was stationed in Yuma, we drove into some Podunk town in West Texas. Best darn ribs I've ever had." Herbie dropped the bare bone onto his dish.

"Better than this?"

"Afraid so." He picked up another rib. "Maybe someday you and I can take a road trip, and see if we can find that place again. Then you can decide for yourself."

Sophia tilted her head to one side and studied the handsome older man before nodding. "You're on."

Even with the spare rib in Herbie's mouth, Sharla could see his smile. It matched the one on her grandmother's face. For the first time ever, Sharla felt like a fifth wheel. Pushing away from the table, she picked up her nearly empty plate. "You two enjoy the rest of your lunch. I'm heading out to see about getting in a little snorkeling."

"See you for dinner, honey." Sophia may have said it, but both she and Herbie were smiling and waving.

To any passerby it would appear they were the nice old couple celebrating fifty years together. If this—whatever—between her grandmother and Herbie lasted past the cruise, Sharla's great-aunts were going to have a cow when they found out he's a retired cop.

For that matter, how would Herbie react to Sophia's past? The thought had Sharla frowning. She didn't think Nana would have told Herbie about her background. What would Herbie say if he knew the family's shady history? She didn't want Nana hurt. *Dang it.* It wasn't Sharla's place to tell him either. All she could do was ride it out. "Blast."

"Something wrong?" Luke stood by the scuba rental shack.

Thinking of her grandmother and Herbie, Sharla hadn't paid any attention to where she was going. Stopping to look around, she realized she'd passed the snorkel hut and had walked pretty far.

Concern creased his forehead. "Is Sophia all right?"

"Oh, yes." She pointed left, then right, then let her hand fall to her side. "Sorry. I wasn't looking where I was going."

"And where were you going?"

"Snorkeling. I think."

"You think?"

She smiled. "It's been eons since I've been on vacation or in the water. At least anything bigger than the neighborhood pool."

"You've been snorkeling before?" Luke had told himself he was going to keep his distance until he'd made up his mind about what to do with the attraction between them. But when he saw her walking with such a deep frown on her face, he couldn't have ignored her any more than he could walk away from a wounded puppy.

"A long time ago. Loved it. I even took scuba lessons, but then…"

"Then?"

She tipped her head and shrugged. "Life got busy."

"How far did you get?"

"With the classes?"

He bobbed his head.

"Open water, but no deeper than twenty-five feet."

"Open water is good. I was just getting ready to go out with the next boat. Want to buddy up?" *So much for distance.* His mouth had opened and the words had simply fallen out.

"Oh, it's been too long. I don't remember—"

"Let's test your memory. Come here." It had taken some convincing on his part to get the scuba rentals to do an afternoon run, but when another two couples walked up wanting the same, the dive captain relented. Most of the equipment was already on the boat and ready to go, but enough remained here for Luke to do a quick run-through with her. See how much she remembered.

"Tell me what this is for?" He held out the pressure gauge.

"That's the gauge that shows how much air I have left."

"And this?"

She glanced a few long seconds at the yellow octo. "That's the backup regulator in case of an emergency, and we need to share air."

Next he lifted the BCD and pointed to the low-pressure inflator.

Her voice a little stronger, she threw out, "Buoyancy Control Device. That's to keep me floating at the surface or buoyant on the bottom."

"Sounds like you're good to go." Together they walked to the back of the small rental shack where a few different wet suits hung. "The water is so warm here, the shorties should do."

Twenty minutes later they were suited up, geared up and sitting side by side on the dive boat riding away from the beach crowd. He could tell by the way her fingers dug into her knees that she was nervous. Maybe he shouldn't have talked her into this. Even if she had been certified years ago, ocean diving was different from a lake or aquarium.

He was all set to tell her coming along wasn't such a great idea, when the boat stopped, and she turned to him with a bright smile "I wouldn't have had the nerve to try this again on my own. Thank you."

Her smile warmed him from the inside out. "You're welcome."

There was no need for any more thinking. He knew what he wanted. Had to try for. Now if he could just keep his hands off of her until he could convince her to give him a chance outside the water.

CHAPTER THIRTEEN

"That was unbelievable." Out of the water and riding back to shore, Sharla shimmied out of the wet suit and stood under the sprayer hose. "Absolutely incredible."

"If you thought that was something, you should see the fish in the Great Barrier Reef. The colors and variety make this place look like a black-and-white photograph."

"I can't imagine." Most of Sharla's scuba lessons had been in a dive shop training pool. Eventually she'd graduated to the lake, but she'd moved to Florida before she'd done any ocean diving. The irony wasn't lost on her. She'd moved to an oceanfront city and never went back in the water. Life had been crazy back then, getting settled in. Then, one by one, her family started migrating south. Soon afterward she'd met land-lover Danny and had never given diving another thought.

Luke took the sprayer from her. "Some buddies and I got a chance to go on leave there, and we grabbed it."

"That's right. You mentioned you'd been in the navy."

The boat sputtered and jerked, then slowed and pulled alongside the short wooden dock.

"All aboard is in thirty minutes," the dive leader said. "You can leave all the rented gear here. We'll take care of it."

Sharla set her face mask on the bench atop the wet suit she'd used, then reached for her cover-up. Sliding it over her head she felt the pockets for her keycard and ID.

"Something wrong?" Luke asked.

"I thought I put my cabin key in the pocket."

Looking first from side to side, he bent down on all

fours, feeling around under the benches.

Her gaze immediately went to the way his swim trunks hugged his backside, and she had to stop her mind from coming up with all sorts of interesting pictures.

"Here you go."

"This seems to be my day to keep saying thank-you." *Especially for the view.* "I wouldn't want to learn the hard way how to get back on the ship without ID."

"I doubt they'd just leave you here."

"Maybe, but I'd rather not find out." If there was one thing she'd gotten good at through the years, it was following the rules. Nothing to attract the attention of the police or a governmental bureaucracy, and that included the ship's captain.

Halfway to the ship, Kyle emerged from under a thatch of palm trees to join them as they walked. "D'ya have a good *dai*?"

"I did." She grinned. He did so sound like an Australian tourism commercial. Any minute she expected him to mention throwing shrimp on the barbie. "Enjoy your afternoon off?"

"Indeed."

He gave a short wave to Luke who, moments ago, had been walking at arm's length beside her and now stood so close she could feel the hair on his arms tickling her skin.

When Kyle fell in step at her other side, Luke's hand slid over and settled at the small of her back. The unexpected contact seared her skin, sending heated sparks in every direction.

As quickly as his hand had advanced, it withdrew. Luke seemed to take an intentional step aside, leaving a good foot of space and no risk of contact between them. It was almost as if he had been as startled as she'd been to find his hand on her back. The rest of the walk he and Kyle chatted about the dive, compared the waters around Australia to the Caribbean and Hawaii, and agreed hands-down that Australia was a winner.

Back on board, keycards recorded and carried-on goods scanned, Kyle waved good-bye to her and Luke, and turned down what she presumed was the crew corridor.

"Sounds like Uncle Sam kept his promise to you," she said.

"Oh, which was that?"

"Join the navy and see the world."

Luke laughed and punched the elevator button. "Oh, yeah. I did at that."

"Did you like it?"

"The navy?"

"Mmm hmm."

"Yes."

"Then why did you leave?" He looked up at the panel of numbers over the elevator for so long that she thought he wasn't going to answer.

"It was time."

She considered the evasion. "What did you do?"

His head turned, and his gaze locked with hers.

The way he stared so intently into her eyes, she'd have believed he was trying to read her mind. Or see her soul.

"I'm a SEAL, Sharla."

There was no need for a mirror to know her eyes were huge with surprise. A million careers in the navy, from paper-pusher to auto mechanic, and he had to be the most elite of Special Forces. "You said 'am' present tense. I thought you weren't in the military anymore?"

"Once a SEAL always a SEAL. But I have been out of the navy for a little over two years."

"Oh." Relief rolled over her like the wake of a speedboat at full throttle. He may have once upon a time been the stuff movies were made of, but he didn't do life-threatening missions anymore. Unless… "So what do you do now?"

"I work for the State Department."

Images of bullets flying and Luke falling on the president to save the commander in chief's life flashed before her eyes in widescreen Technicolor. "Secret Service?" She hoped he didn't hear the note of panic in her voice.

"No." He smiled. "The president's going to have to stay

safe without me."

The tension eased from her shoulders. She wasn't looking for a man and a relationship, but something about Luke Chapman was so darn hard to resist. But resist she would if he'd had another high-risk job. She'd been there. Done that. Hated the T-shirt. "Then what do you do?"

He hesitated again, studying her much the way he had a few minutes before, when she had asked what he'd done in the navy. "Internal Affairs."

"Ooh, that's gotta be rough. I know in the police department, those guys might as well work in a leper colony." The night Danny had died, Tyler had taken out the perp with one clean shot. While the rest of the department had cheered, Internal Affairs had run an investigation. Standard procedure, Tyler had told her. But she saw how it had affected him and the other guys who had been mulling about her house in those days.

"Someone has to do it." Luke smiled but the usual sparkle didn't appear in his eyes.

The elevator opened at her floor, and she wasn't surprised to have Luke follow her out and down the hall to her cabin to wait while she shoved open the door.

Over her shoulder he did a quick visual, and this time his eyes twinkled brightly when he smiled at her. "See you at dinner."

She was going to have to make up her mind. Even if Luke didn't have a high-risk job, and regardless how he seemed—with every hour—to dig himself deeper under her skin, he wasn't likely to be looking for a relationship anyhow.

The cabin steward had already left her a new folded-towel animal on the bed. A peacock. She almost laughed. Beautiful and captivating. Just like Luke Chapman.

Seated at the head of the table, Herbie dropped his napkin and, leaning over, whispered to Luke. "Anything new?"

Luke gave a minimal shake of his head. There'd been no time to contact Kate. On land he'd kept his cell on Roam just in case she had some breaking news for him. But nothing. They'd have to wait for the music trivia contest tonight and try to get George talking after the game.

"Oh, look." Sophia broke away from her conversation with Sharla and waved her fingers in the air.

His back to the door, Luke saw no need to turn and look. Gloria Bailey's perfume smacked him upside the head twenty seconds before she reached the table.

"So glad you decided to join us." Sophia smiled at Gloria and George, then glanced over to Herbie and Luke. "We bumped into each other in the ladies' room a little while ago."

"We have the most boring table." Gloria took an empty seat. "One honeymoon couple who can't stop making goo-goo eyes long enough to chew, never mind talk. And two sisters from Wyoming. I didn't know people really lived there. All they talk about is sheep. Ack."

"So naturally I said they should join us, since we have these two extra chairs." Sophia beamed a little too brightly for a mere friendly gesture.

The same gut feeling Luke had when Conway had talked him into taking this cruise reared its head. Sophia's grin shouted ulterior motive. But what in heaven's name could the old bird want with George and Gloria?

Sophia and Herbie moved over a place so George could sit by his wife. In no time at all George and Herbie were already engrossed in sports talk, but Luke knew Herbie was just waiting for an opening. Gloria on the other hand seemed to have a mind only for food. For a thin woman, she ate like the proverbial horse. She'd ordered two appetizers, the salad, and the New York strip steak with grilled shrimp.

He couldn't tell if Sharla's eyes were wide from the amount of food Gloria had ordered or the size of the rock Gloria kept waving in front of Sharla's face. An inch closer and she could take out an eye with the thing.

Sophia seemed to be the only one engrossed in the tiny menu, but he'd noticed her gaze shift from the specials to the hand Gloria kept waving about as her mouth prattled on about the secret to weight control being the right balance of protein, carbs and fat. He suspected a good plastic surgeon was probably her true secret weapon but thought it safer to refrain from commenting. He also debated if Sophia's interest was in her granddaughter's safety or the size of the ring that had almost smacked him in the face as well, on that first day on the ship.

Ordering only the salad and the Chilean bass, Sophia gave the waiter that sweet doting smile that made Luke think of lilacs and crocheted afghans and all things granny, then she looked up at George. "So, what are your and Gloria's plans for when we dock in San Juan tomorrow?"

The way George puffed up before speaking, Luke already knew George was going to start bragging on his real estate ventures.

"Actually I'm going to hire a car and head out to the site of my next project."

"Oh, Herbie mentioned you're in real estate. Such an interesting business, but I have such a terrible head for numbers. I'd never be able to understand it."

"Not what I do."

"Why is that?"

"Well, we all know the real money to be made is in the resort land deals. There are so many small investors who can't amass enough funds to buy into a large opportunity alone, but together..." He raised a forefinger at her and winked. "Together they can play with the big boys."

"You make it sound more like fun than business. What part in this dealmaking do you have?" Sophia leaned back for the waiter to set her salad in front of her. The entire table remained quiet as the two servers set a dish before each of them.

As soon as the waitstaff were gone, George continued his explanation. "I keep an eye out for underdeveloped property with resort potential. Many Caribbean islands have limited economies in the main cities and ports, but, with the right backing, private resorts in the outskirts become popular tourist destinations."

"Especially the ones for honeymoons," Gloria added between bites of her escargot.

"Then what?" Sophia pressed.

"A corporation is formed and investors put money into a pool in exchange for shares in the new company. Those funds are then used to buy small parcels of land at a good price. Once all the parcels are bought up, the corporation sells the land as a package to the developers for a nice profit."

Luke saw the opening to get more info and pounced. "You've found a good site in San Juan?"

"Not San Juan proper of course. On the east side of the island."

Not wanting to seem too interested, Luke paused, stabbing at a lettuce leaf. "Really? Why is this site a contender?"

"Pristine beaches. Off the beaten path, but not too far from the main highway. Building roads and bringing in infrastructure will be done at a minimal cost. Big companies put the local sugar cane growers out of business long ago. The nearby small village is dying, and the descendants are ready to move on to bigger and better things. The timing is right."

Sophia cut into her fish. "Sounds perfect."

"It really is. The locals call it Miracle Bend. Back in the late eighteen hundreds, an epidemic of what historians believe might have been typhoid fever hit that side of the island. There used to be a small catholic monastery nearby. They took in the sick, instructed the locals in the then-unheard-of practices of boiling for sterilization, and washing their hands before handling food and water. The spread of the disease slowed, the sick began to recover and, as far as the locals were concerned, the monks saved the people and the economy. Which at the time relied heavily on having enough people to work the sugar cane."

"Great story." Herbie pointed to George with his fork. "Tourists love local color. Too bad I didn't bump into George here sooner. All the company shares have been sold."

Sophia blew out a heavy sigh, her entire body deflating with the departed breath. "Well, that's just a shame. I've had a little money tucked away looking for the right investment, and this seems like the perfect fit for me. I have the money, and you have the brains."

Saint George blustered and grinned. "You are too kind."

"I've had almost a hundred grand sitting in the bank earning pennies for so long, maybe you can keep me in mind for your next project?"

For a few seconds George's complexion grew so pale, Luke wondered if Sophia had just given the man a heart attack, but, before anyone else noticed his reaction, George cleared his throat and leaned slightly forward over his empty plate. "If you two would like to tag along tomorrow and see for yourselves, I can have the accountant double-check all the files and confirm we're sold out."

"Ooh." Sophia clapped her hands together excitedly. "Wouldn't that be wonderful, Herbie, if there were a few more shares available?"

Herbie's gaze bore into Sophia. "Yes. Yes it would."

CHAPTER FOURTEEN

Something was going on, and, though Sharla didn't have a clue what, she was positive she didn't like it. Since when did Nana have a hundred grand sitting in the bank collecting dust? The whole reason they shared a house was to cut back on expenses. And what was all this business about real estate? Why in heaven's name would her grandmother want to buy into a resort? Of all the things… *Oh, no!*

Surely after all these years her grandmother wasn't coming out of retirement. To the best of Sharla's knowledge, her grandmother hadn't been involved in a real con since Grandpa had died. How Sharla wished she'd paid more attention to the stories. What were all the cons? The Shell Game, The Wire, The Pay Up… or was it Payoff? *Blast.*

And which the heck one involved buying into land development deals? Except… wasn't it usually the crook who offered up the phony sale, not the other way around? But there were all sorts of cons where the grifter pretended to offer up a ton of cash to get what they wanted from the mark. Look at all the stupid Internet scams about inherited millions from a country no one ever heard of.

What she needed was a deep breath and a stiff drink. After all the games and entertainment tonight, when they got back to the cabin, she'd just ask Nana what was what. That's all. Nice and simple.

"Sharla?"

She felt the warmth of Luke's hand on her arm before she heard her name. That was twice today that the slightest of his touches had her full attention. "Hmm?"

"I'm skipping dessert. Have a couple of things to see to before trivia tonight." His hand remained in place, and, when she hesitated while her mind struggled to process his words, his thumb moved back and forth with the barest of caresses. "You okay?"

Dropping her gaze to watch his finger graze across her wrist, she realized she didn't want him to stop. Didn't want him to get up and leave. Forcing herself to raise her gaze to meet his, the depth of concern she found in his eyes slammed into her like a middle linebacker. She nodded, afraid to speak. Afraid of the words that might slip through the filters in her brain.

His thumb stopped moving, but his hand didn't move. "You sure?"

"Yes," she mumbled softly.

Hesitantly he pulled away, and she stopped herself from snatching his hand back. Made herself look toward the others. Wondered how everyone else could be chatting so completely unaware of the energy sparking between her and Luke. And stumped by what to do about it.

During the entire walk from the dining room to the computer stations, Luke failed to push Sharla from his thoughts. Something had been bothering her. He didn't have to be a mind reader to know that much. What he did know was that he didn't like seeing her worried or upset. And that got him thinking about what had caused the little dip in her brow which told him that she wasn't lost in happy thoughts.

Seated at the computer, he typed a message to Kate.

LUKE: Got more info. Possible previous deals in Fiji and Barbados. Current deal east of San Juan.

Kate's dialogue box popped up. *Hi, there.*

LUKE: Hi. How goes it?

KATE: Fine. Some muckety-muck is up Conway's butt. He doesn't have time to notice a little side work. ☺

LUKE: Good. This new place, the locals call it Miracle

Bend. Something about monks and typhoid fever. Used to be sugar cane fields.

KATE: Okay… got it!

LUKE: Knew you would, babe.

KATE: Officially it's Puerto de Nueva Granada, the harbor for the abandoned village Nueva Granada.

LUKE: So I heard. Who owns the land?

KATE: Let's see.

He stared at the blank screen willing the right words to flash before him.

KATE: Hmm. I'm going to need some time to dig a little deeper.

LUKE: What is it? As if he expected the guy to be legit.

KATE: Unless your guy is the department of agriculture…

LUKE: Definitely not.

KATE: Let me dig. There's some weird stuff here about surfers.

Surfers?

LUKE: OK. I'll check back later.

KATE: See ya!

LUKE: Thanks again.

KATE: Anything for that smile!

And before he could type *Back at you,* she was gone.

By the time he made it to the lounge for trivia, his five tablemates were ready to play and had saved him a seat. Next to Sharla.

With a smile, Sophia handed him a spare pencil. "Thought you were going to miss the start. Hope you're a Michael Jackson fan."

"Never miss a date with you." He grinned back. Truth was, he was enjoying the games just as much as Sophia. Even if they weren't a matter of life or death. "We'll have to see about Michael."

The first tune had most people in the room under forty scratching their heads.

Sophia immediately wrote "Rocking Robin."

When a few of the younger folks were stumped, they protested that wasn't a Michael Jackson song. Becky, the brunette from the cruise staff, explained tonight's contest included hits from the Jackson Five. The frowns abounding in the crowd indicated they were not pleased with the prospect.

Luke had to laugh. All this fuss over winning a key chain or highlighter. Now if they were giving free drinks…

Between the four of them—Sophia, Sharla, Gloria and him—they should have nailed them all. That is if Gloria knew her Michael Jackson as well as she had claimed.

Herbie and George were doing their best to carry on a conversation without annoying Sophia.

Though Luke tried to keep one ear on the two men's talk, he was having more fun dissecting the first five notes of some of the biggest hits of the nineties.

Fifteen minutes later Sophia was doing her winning shimmies, and the six of them had cruise line money belts.

Luke still didn't get why the cruise line didn't just give out vouchers for a free drink. The company had to know most of these prizes were going to wind up in a trash can between here and the passengers' kitchens back home.

"Now where to?" Gloria seemed more excited tonight than any other night.

And she deserved it. She'd been right on the six songs that had the rest of them stumped. The woman knew her Michael Jackson. She'd turned out to be smarter than Luke had expected about a lot of the trivia. Tonight they'd been the only team to get all twenty tunes correct.

"I vote for craps." Sophia raised her fists and shook her shoulders. "I'm feeling lucky."

Herbie glanced over, and Luke was pretty sure he saw the guy salivating. Herbie clearly had it bad for the feisty old bird. And Luke couldn't blame Herbie. If Luke had been fifteen years older, and Sophia fifteen years younger, he'd have fallen for her himself. Though it gave him a good picture of what to expect with Sharla in thirty or forty years.

Thirty or forty years? Was that what he wanted?

Shaking her head at her grandmother, Sharla had undone the plastic wrapping, extended the strap, and hung the versatile pouch from her neck. "I vote for the show. We haven't seen one yet."

"Tonight's the comedian. I heard he's pretty good." Herbie said this more to Sophia than the group.

"Nope," Sophia responded. "I don't want to sit in a chair and watch. I want to participate." She whipped out her trusty daily report. "I suppose we could do poolside bingo after dark."

"I love bingo." Gloria rubbed her hands together. "Besides, I'm with Sophia. I'm feeling lucky."

"Then I guess bingo it is." Herbie held his arm out to Sophia, George followed suit, and Luke stared at Sharla.

The next thirty years of his life were running through his mind in fast forward, and, try as he might, none of it seemed right without Sharla. He slowly extended his elbow to her. "Shall we join them?"

Sliding her hand into the crook of his arm, she flashed that smile that felt like warm sunshine. "At least it's not craps."

He wasn't so sure about that. Something told him that, if he tossed the dice and went after Sharla tonight with the life he had now, he'd roll snake eyes.

The lounge emptied quickly. Many of the trivia players hurried to the late-night dinner seating. Others left in search of who-knew-what. Only a few settled in for another drink and the soft sounds of the famous crooners from the fifties flowing from the sound system.

Having led the way, George and Gloria were already out of sight. Herbie and Sophia were at the top of the three steps exiting the lounge when Sharla's grip on his arm tightened, her eyes widening.

Before Luke could see what had stopped Sharla, a hard thud sounded across the room followed by a loud smack.

"Oh, no." Sharla's gaze settled on a stunned man standing over a puddle of a woman at his feet. "Did you hear her head hit?"

Everyone should have heard the sound. A nearby waiter stopped to look in the couple's direction, but Becky, the staff member, was surrounded by a small group of chatty passengers oblivious to the accident.

Sharla had already changed trajectory when the man leaned over, arms outstretched, obviously about to move his wife away from the bottom of the stairs.

"No!" Sharla screamed loud enough for the man to hear and to pierce a few eardrums as well. Letting go of Luke's arm, she bolted over a stool and around the meandering passengers, landing at the older woman's side before her husband could touch her. "You don't want to move her."

Luke's instincts had been the same as Sharla's. He'd practically sailed across the room after her, when the guy had tried to move his wife. Luke might not be a medic or trauma nurse, but even he knew the risks of moving an injured person.

Bending down, Sharla did a quick assessment and hollered across to Becky, "She's out cold. Call the doctor." Then she placed one hand on the woman's chest while she checked for a pulse with the other.

The woman's husband stood paralyzed, watching Sharla examine his wife.

"She's breathing fine and the pulse, although weak and thready, is palpable." Glancing up at the woman's husband, she asked, "Does your wife have a history of falling?"

He shook his head.

"Dizzy spells?"

Another head shake. "No. Nothing. Her doctor says she's as healthy as a woman ten years younger."

"That's a good thing." Sharla smiled again. Within seconds the woman began to stir. "Don't move," Sharla practically cooed. When the woman's eyes shot open wide, Sharla cupped her cheek with one hand, casually keeping her head from moving, and turned to Becky shouting orders like a drill sergeant. "Make sure the medical team brings a backboard and a neck stabilizer."

Immediately her voice reverted to a soft soothing tone. "You've had a little fall. Does it hurt anywhere?"

The woman closed her eyes and barely shook her head.

"That's good. What's your name?"

The husband, still frozen in place, opened his mouth to answer, but Luke held up his hand, shaking his head. He knew Sharla was checking for a head injury and needed the wife to respond, not her husband.

Opening her eyes, the woman softly answered, "Agnes."

Sharla looked to Agnes' husband, her relief showing when he nodded. "Nice to meet you, Agnes. Do you know where you are?"

"Ship," she mumbled.

"That's right." Reaching for both of Agnes' hands, she commanded, "I need you to squeeze as hard as you can."

When the woman did as instructed, Sharla asked the surrounding crowd if anyone had a smart phone. Accepting one of the three quickly proffered phones, she turned on the flashlight. After checking the woman's eyes, one at a time, Sharla glanced up at the husband, still as pale as her patient. "Her grip is good, and her pupils react equally. The ship's doctor will take her down to the treatment room, and check for fractures and internal injuries, but I don't think she's been hurt too badly. They'll probably want to observe her overnight to be sure." She stood and patted his back. "She'll be in good hands."

The woman smiled at Sharla and lifted her hand.

Sharla crouched back down and clasped it between both of hers. "Everything will be fine. You'll see."

The woman's eyelids fell shut just as the doctor arrived and knelt at her side.

After pulling out his stethoscope from the black bag he'd brought, he listened to her heartbeat for a few seconds before looking to Sharla. "What happened?"

"She slipped down the stairs. Hit her head pretty hard and was out for at least two or three minutes. Her pulse was weak and thready, but it's stronger now."

"And she's coherent?" he asked.

"Yes. Knows her name and where she is. Pupils react, and her grip is strong. Didn't have a chance to do much else."

No longer needed, Luke stepped away from the huddle.

Sharla remained in place, allowing the staff to do their thing. At one point, not pleased with something, she nudged aside the crew member and placed the neck brace on the patient herself. Once Agnes was on the gurney to Sharla's satisfaction, she smiled at the doctor and took a step back.

Agnes lifted up her hand again. Sharla leaned over, and a bright smile took over her face before she nodded and stepped completely out of the way.

"What did she say?" Luke sidled up beside her, his hands on her arms.

He was so very proud of her, anyone would think she'd saved a battalion of men.

"Just thank-you." She kept her eyes on the crew rolling Agnes toward the elevators.

"Awfully big smile for getting a thank-you."

"It's always nice to hear. Poor thing was just so embarrassed to have fallen."

"Is she going to be all right?"

"They'll want to observe her overnight to make sure she doesn't have a problem with bleeding into the brain. But she's probably more embarrassed than hurt."

"You were wonderful."

Sharla turned to look at him. "It was just a little fall."

"I know. But it was a big deal to Agnes and her husband. You were all business and comforting and reassuring at the same time. That means a lot to someone when you're hurting. And scared."

"The voice of experience?" She used the same words he had the other night on deck.

He just nodded. Too many memories of too many good men hurt and dying flashed before his eyes. Along with the medics, risking their own lives to save their buddies and too often failing. This may not be a Middle East desert, but this woman had the heart of warrior. And an angel.

Finally able to wind down from the unexpected medical emergency, Sharla found playing evening bingo had turned out to be way more fun than she'd imagined.

They'd sat around in deck chairs watching the numbers appear on the big screen over the pool. The cruise staff guy, Insk from Minsk, was calling the numbers and making ridiculous jokes in an absurd version of what she suspected was a Russian accent. "What's written at the bottom of a milk bottle in Minsk?" he asked. After a long pause he answered, "Open other end." As stupid as the shtick was, he had her laughing so hard a few times, tears would stream down her cheeks.

"Okay." Nana set down her cards. She hadn't won big, but she'd won back some of her bingo fees. "Now it's time for the crap tables. But I need to get my money from the cabin. Why don't you kids come with us?"

It wasn't an order, but it wasn't a question either.

Nana turned to Gloria and George. "We'll meet you at the tables?"

"I'll be at the slots," Gloria answered.

"Blackjack's my game," George added.

"Sounds like a plan. See you in a few." Nana linked arms with Sharla, clearly expecting her to come along. Herbie and Luke shrugged and fell into step behind them.

In the elevator everyone remained silent as passengers moving about loaded on and off at every other floor. When they reached the cabin, Herbie took Nana's keycard and opened the door for everyone. Herbie did the same thing as Luke, quickly glancing about just in case the Boston Strangler was hiding out in Nana and Sharla's room.

She lifted her hand to her mouth to hide her laughter.

Everyone stood aimlessly in the small space as Nana took her position in front of the cabinetry with the small safe.

The moment the cabin door latched shut, Nana spun around and pointed a finger at Herbie and Luke. "What in blazes kind of game are you two hustlers up to?"

CHAPTER FIFTEEN

Herbie's jaw dropped; Luke's brows shot to his hairline, and Sharla was aghast. "Nana!"

"Don't *Nana* me, young lady. Sit down."

On command, Sharla obediently dropped to the edge of the bed. Herbie snapped his mouth shut. Luke tossed a sideways glance at him, and both men shifted to sit.

"Not you two," Nana ordered. "I want answers."

Luke looked to Herbie and lifted a shoulder in a casual shrug.

"Well?"

"I'm afraid we' don't know what you're talking about," Herbie said.

"What crazy stunt are you two trying to pull with that half-assed con artist?"

"What?" Sharla shot up. *This couldn't be good.*

"Honey, this is between these two. You'd better sit down."

"Nana, I don't think—"

"It's okay, honey. I know what I'm doing."

"Sophia," Herbie spoke first. "I'm sure you've misunderstood."

"The hell I have. *It takes a con to spot a con* may be true most of the time, but, this time, any idiot should be able to smell this guy's stink a mile away."

Luke's brows went up again, and Sharla swallowed a groan.

"Have either of you asked for an accounting report?"

Both shook their heads.

"What about references? Real ones, not testimonials."

Herbie shot another quick glance at Luke before

volunteering, "Not exactly."

"Care to expand on that?"

Again his head shifted from side to side. Obviously not ready to explain further.

"Well, I know neither of you are stupid. Crazy maybe, but not stupid." She turned to Herbie. "You're an ex-cop. Didn't you work vice?"

Herbie nodded.

"And you." She pointed a finger at Luke. "Sharla says you work for the State Department."

Luke swallowed and bobbed his head.

"In other words, CIA."

Again that wasn't a question, and Sharla's heart took off at a rapid clip. She put one hand on her chest and the other on Nana's arm, Her grandmother knew an awful lot of strange things about a world Sharla never even thought about, but she had to be wrong about Luke.

His gaze shifted to Sharla for a few very long seconds before he turned back to her grandmother. "I can neither confirm nor deny."

Luke was glad Sharla was already sitting down. The way her face went pale as the sheets on the bed, he suspected, had she been standing, she might have keeled over.

He'd considered falling on standard operating procedure and denying outright that he worked for The Company. Evading the way he had earlier with Sharla. But now that the idea of a lifetime with Sharla had started to take root in his mind, he couldn't bring himself to put up any more smoke screens. He just wished she didn't look so horrified.

"So." Sophia slid her hands onto her hips. "Now that we've established that neither of you are neophytes, what's the plan with this character, and why are we after him?"

"We're not after anything," Herbie took a step in Sophia's direction.

She held up her hand to stop him. "There are a few things I haven't gotten around to explaining to you yet, Herbie."

"Nana." Sharla seemed to snap out of her slight daze. "I don't think now is—"

"I'm afraid now is as good a time as any." She reached over and patted her granddaughter's cheek, then turned back to the men. "I come from a long line of confidence men."

Con artists?

Herbie's brows buckled, and he took a step back.

"My husband Benny and I retired when my daughter married a reputable archeologist. It wouldn't have looked good for my son-in-law's career to have his wife's family caught up in a major scandal."

No doubt a euphemism for *jail.*

"Most of our relatives retired shortly after that. All the newfangled technology and gizmos took a lot of the fun out of it anyway."

Herbie took a seat next to Sharla.

Luke couldn't blame him. The news was a bit of a shocker, but, instead of feeling weak in the knees, he found himself stifling a smile. No wonder the old bird was so feisty.

"None of that is important now," Sophia continued. "What's important is this guy is a con. And not a good one either. And you want him. So tell me what you're up to, and then we'll see how I can help."

"Nana."

"Okay, how *we* can help."

"Nana!"

Herbie stared at Sophia for a long while.

Sharla seemed to be floundering from incensed to mortified and back, and Luke was at a complete loss for words. He'd run a lot of missions in his day, done a great deal of undercover work over the last two years, but, he had to admit, running a con was not his forte.

"Would you two excuse us for a little bit?" Herbie pushed to his feet. "I'd like to talk with Sophia alone. We'll meet you in the casino soon."

Sharla looked to her grandmother, who smiled. "It will be fine, honey. You and Luke go win some money."

Silence hung in the air for a bit. He was pretty sure Sharla was going to object when Sophia patted her arm and repeated, "Go." After another minute of consideration, Sharla turned and led Luke to the door.

Neither said a word in the hall. In the elevator he was surprised when she pushed the button for the upper deck instead of the casino. He didn't know what to say. Finally he said the only thing he could think of. "I really like Sophia."

"I love her."

"I know you do."

Sharla kept her gaze on the closed elevator doors. "I don't want her to get hurt."

"Believe it or not, neither do I."

The doors opened, and he followed her out to the upper deck and jogging path they'd walked the other night. Not a bad idea. He could use a little fresh air.

"Do you really work for the CIA?"

Lips pressed together, he took a chance. "Yes."

"Why did you lie?"

"I didn't."

She stopped and faced him. "You said you were with Internal Affairs."

"In a way I am." When she didn't say anything or resume walking, he added, "Every agency has its problems with rotten apples. I've been working to help get rid of a few."

She returned to following the path. "Did you?"

Gazing out at the stars, he thought of the three dead bodies in the luxury compound in Afghanistan. "Yes."

They continued walking around the front and out of the wind. "What happens when your thirty days' leave are up? Do you go back to finding more bad apples?"

And wasn't that one hell of a question. Five days ago he would have said *of course, yes*. Even this morning he would have said yes. But ever since picturing the two of them old and happy in thirty years, he wasn't so sure. "Honestly I don't know."

Once again she stopped short, turned to him and studied his face a good while before asking, "Why?"

"Because of you."

Of all the answers he could have given her, that wasn't what Sharla had expected. She kept walking. Without a word they rounded the path more than once. She wasn't sure if it was twice or even three or four times. She had no idea.

As they turned the corner into the strong breeze at the front of the ship, his hand slid over and grabbed hold of hers. Their fingers wove together and, instead of the usual shock of electricity that his touch brought, a sense of comfort and strength blanketed her like an old quilt on a winter's night. A sense of belonging so solid that it overwhelmed her, robbing her of words.

She had no idea what to do or say.

Could she do this again? Could she take a chance on falling in love with another man with a high-risk career? Just the thought squeezed at her heart. And the possibility she was already on her way tightened the pressure. "I thought it was a nightmare." She dared a glance at Luke, his face void of all emotion. His gaze straight ahead. "Tyler came to tell me what happened. There was no time to rush to the hospital and worry over a wounded husband in intensive care. Danny was already gone at the scene. We'd only been married three years. But we were happy."

In her peripheral vision she could see Luke nodding.

"I don't want to care about what might happen to you. And I don't think I could live with the fear."

Squeezing her hand, he shifted his attention to her. "I don't want you to live in fear of anything."

They made one more lap around the deck when, still holding her hand, Luke paused by the doorway leading inside. "It's getting late. Sophia and Herbie might be looking for us."

"Right."

All the way to the casino he kept hold of her hand and not once had she felt the need to pull away. Inside with the smoke and noises associated with gambling, they walked from the crap tables to the blackjack tables. Finding Gloria by the slot machines.

"Have you seen Nana or Herbie?"

"Nope. George waited for about an hour and then went to bed. I hadn't gotten up to look, but I'm sure I would have noticed them if they'd come in." From her vantage point she certainly could have seen them at the craps table.

"Then, I guess I'll see you tomorrow. Good luck." Sharla flashed a thumbs-up with her free hand.

Back in the game, Gloria managed to wiggle a two-fingered goodbye.

"Where to now?" Luke asked.

"My room. Hopefully Nana isn't curled up crying her eyes out."

To her surprise one side of Luke's mouth lifted in a sly smile. "I'd be more worried about Herbie."

Considering how concerned she was about her grandmother, she shouldn't have felt like smiling too, but she did. Luke was probably right. Her grandmother was many things, and a force to be reckoned with was at the top of the list.

Still holding her hand, Luke's pace slowed as they moved down the hallway. "Uh-oh."

Not seeing anything out of the ordinary, her heart pounding against her ribs, she faced Luke. "What?"

"That." Several feet from her room, he drew to a stop and pointed at the door.

"That's odd. Why is Nana's scarf tied to the doorknob?"

Luke turned to her with brows raised.

It's a good thing he looked totally irresistible when he did that or it might start to get annoying.

"Back in the day, did your grandmother ever work the resorts in the Catskills or Poconos?"

"Now that you mention it, I think the family did, when she was a kid, before she married my grandpa. The

Catskills. Why?"

In a move worthy of a ballroom dancer, his hand slipped from hers to around her waist and redirected her back up the hall. "Come on, and I'll explain."

Alone together in the elevator he pushed the button to his floor, and her already-racing heart nearly sputtered to a stop. "We're going to your room?"

"We are if you want to get any sleep tonight." His grip on her side eased, and he blew out a resigned breath. "Surely you've seen the movie *Dirty Dancing*."

"One of my favorites."

"Do you remember the scene when the sister found a towel on the doorknob of the guy's cabin?"

"Yeah, that's when she walked in on—Oh. My. God."

CHAPTER SIXTEEN

He had no idea what was going through Sharla's mind as they made their way to his cabin. When he pushed open the door and waited for her to step past him, to go inside, he could see her studying the contents of the room. Indecision showing in every line of her tense stance.

"It's perfectly safe. I promise." Extending his hand to her was not an option right now. Touching her in anyway would be a big mistake. Especially if he wanted to keep the promise he'd just made.

With the slightest of nods, she crossed the threshold. "I don't even have a toothbrush."

Smothering a chuckle, he quickly turned away to close the door. "It's too late to call the steward in here, but I'm sure we can separate the beds on our own."

The way her head spun around so fast he almost thought she'd seen a rat. The four-legged kind. Avoiding getting too close to her, he walked to the other side of the bed and lifted the blanket.

"Here. Let me help." Standing by the opposite corner, she pulled at the other end, folded it in her arms and held it out to him. "Where shall I put this?"

"Probably under the beds once I pull them apart." He reached out to take hold of the neatly folded spread, and their fingers brushed ever-so-slightly against each other. Her head shot up, and she pinned him with her gaze. The sparks flying between them were as real as the electrical current powering the overhead lights. And just as shocking. All he needed to do was take a step back. Okay, two steps. Drawing on every ounce of willpower he possessed, he eased his way back to the wall. Ignoring the sound of her footsteps as she set the blanket on a nearby chair, he grabbed the pillows and tossed them over his shoulder across the small room. When he turned around, she'd piled the pillows on the blanket and was moving back to help with the linens. A flat top sheet in one hand, he pulled at the bottom sheet when she sidled up to him. "I'll fold that."

"Thanks."

Once again their hands touched and sparks flew, this couldn't go on.

Forcing his hands to his sides at this very moment was probably one of the hardest things he'd ever done. Rearranging the room would be easier without her distracting him. Leaving the beds as they were for now, he opened a nearby drawer and pulled out the biggest t-shirt he owned. Tonight he would sleep in his clothes. An ounce of prevention and all that. "Why don't you see if this will work for a pajama and I'll finish rearranging the beds."

The way her gaze dropped to the t-shirt and over to the bed, he wondered if she was thinking maybe an all night casino session would be a better alternative. The thought had crossed his mind too. Then again, he was a SEAL who'd survived hell week, he could spend the night with a beautiful woman and keep his hands to himself. Besides they had a big day ahead of them tomorrow and for her own safety he didn't need her falling asleep on her feet.

"I'll be right back." Slowly, she pivoted on her heel, and taking two small steps, let herself into the bathroom.

He needed to focus. First the two beds needed to be separated. Removing the pad that held them together, he dumped it on the pile of pillows, and shoved the beds apart with a little more force than was necessary. With the two beds neatly tucked against opposite walls, Brooklyn surveyed his work. Though it made no sense, somehow having two dorm style beds in the cabin instead of one big bed made him breathe a little easier. As long as he didn't get within touching distance he'd be just fine. And if he repeated that often enough, maybe by morning he'd believe it.

The bathroom door creaked open and Sharla inched her way back into the tiny cabin. She looked so darn cute in his Go Navy t-shirt. Since he usually used it for working out, it was pretty big on him. On her the thing was a tent. Almost to her knees it hid more that her bathing suit cover-up, but he could still see her blushing from her collarbone to her rosy red cheeks.

"You look absolutely gorgeous." The words slipped out. How in an oversized T-shirt and bare feet she managed to be the most beautiful woman he'd ever seen, he didn't know—and didn't care. Best behavior and all, right now he didn't want to be anywhere else.

"Thank you." Her gaze shifted to the now separated beds and pile of linens. "Oh, I'll make the beds."

He shifted left, she shifted right and came within inches of a full body collision. In a discombobulated effort to separate, she turned left instead and spinning in the opposite direction as well, he nearly knocked her over.

"Oops, sorry," she mumbled.

"No. That was my fault." Pivoting away, he carefully held his hands at his sides repeating the mantra, *do not touch*. Dancing around her in an awkward effort to keep his hands—and body—to himself, instead of easily crossing the small space, they bumped into the two night tables now sitting in the middle of the room and sending them bouncing into the dresser. Which in turn had Sharla stepping back and hitting her head against the bathroom door.

All thoughts of keeping his distance fled. Brooklyn reached forward. Ignoring the no touch rule he'd imposed on himself, he lightly brushed his hand against her temple. "I'm sorry, are you okay?"

If she'd wanted to she'd have been well in her rights to yell at him for knocking into her, or grumble about an impending headache. To his surprise, as soon as the shock of impact fell away, Sharla burst out laughing.

Shaking her head, she winced at the movement, and rubbing the side of her head where she'd collided with the door, she swallowed another laugh. "Don't we make quite the pair?"

She was right. They were being ridiculous.

Brooklyn chuckled and nodded. "Let me help with the bed."

Smiling again, she let her hand fall to her side. "If you dare."

"Never dare a SEAL."

Sharla rolled her eyes and laughed again. Tension gone, working together they had the single bed tended in no time. The oversized sheets, tucked over double.

"What about the other bed?" she asked.

Brooklyn kicked off his shoes, grabbed a pillow, tossed it at the head of the unmade bed and sat. "I'll use this one."

The way her brows furrowed, anyone would think he'd told her he was going to sleep outdoors in a snow bank.

"I'll be fine. It's too late to bother the steward. Besides," he laid back, locked his fingers behind his head and crossed his ankles. "I couldn't be more comfortable."

"Right." Hands on her hips she looked around the room, her gaze settling back on the other bed. "We'll each take one sheet and fold it double like a sleeping bag."

Not waiting for an answer, she spun around and yanked at one corner of the bed sheets.

"Hey," he sprang to his feet. "You're messing with my hospital corners."

"You can't sleep on a bare mattress."

He stood behind her, close enough to smell her perfume, or maybe it was just her shampoo. "Why not?"

Holding on to one corner of the sheet, she craned her neck over her shoulder to look at him. "What do you mean why not?"

"I mean." He turned her to face him. "Why can I not sleep on a bare mattress?"

"Because," her brows dipped in that cute little frown he liked, "you just aren't supposed to do that."

He wanted to argue with her some more. Make her see the illogic in her logic, but with her brows crinkled adorably and her mouth slightly open preparing her next point, he simply couldn't resist anymore. Ignoring the mantra repeating on a never ending loop in the back of his mind, he brought his lips down on hers.

After the initial awkwardness of finding herself confined in such a small space with the one man who had gotten completely under her skin, she'd thought she'd found solid footing with him…until now.

His lips danced, teased, and almost taunted her. Strong hands remained cemented at her waist. Like a rich dessert, the kiss was sweet and supple to be slowly savored for as long as she could. When his hands slipped away and she felt him easing back, she came within inches of curling her arms around his neck and dragging him back for more.

"We should get some sleep. Tomorrow is going to be a long day."

"Mm," she mumbled, her mind reliving the last moments. Not until he stopped his retreat, did she realize she'd reached out and snatched hold of his hand.

His gaze dropped to their laced fingers.

"That was nice," she said softly.

"Very," his voice was low, and rough, and wrapped around her like a warm embrace. "But you need to get some rest."

"Right. Rest." Closing her eyes, she nodded and never letting go, stepped back, her legs hitting the bed, knocking her clumsily onto the mattress and bringing him tumbling down beside her. Expecting him any second to pull away and bolt cross the room to his own bed, she was surprised to have him lift the corner of the sheet for her to slide under cover.

Pressing his back to the wall, he gently placed the sheet and blanket across her, spooned her into his side, and kissing her temple, softly whispered. "Good night."

The feeling of sheer joy that ricocheted through Brooklyn's system when Sharla laced her fingers in his took him completely by surprise. The simple gesture created a connection so deep and strong that not even a meteor crashing into the ship could have dragged him away from her side.

His heart had kicked into double time when rather than pull away or question him, she'd snuggled into his side for the night. She didn't know it yet, but he did. No matter his job or his past, or hers, he'd finally come home.

"Everything's Coming up Roses" sounded loudly. Sharla shifted, bumping into a hard warm surface. Luke. He'd kept his promise. She'd been more than safe. Tucked into the fold of his arms, she was the happiest and most at home she'd been a very very long time.

Breathing in her ear, he mumbled, "Your phone is ringing."

The last thing Sharla wanted was to break the spell and let in the real world. "It can't be my phone. We're in the middle of the ocean."

"Not anymore." His arm shifted around her waist and tugged her closer in the already narrow space. "We've docked in Puerto Rico. US territory. All our phones will work."

"Oh."

"It could be Sophia."

Nana. She didn't even want to think about what her grandmother and Herbie were up to, or what they must think she and Luke were doing. All she wanted was stay wrapped in his arms until the ship returned to home port.

"You should check." His hold on her barely loosened.

"I know." She resisted the urge to plant one small kiss on those delicious lips and instead crawled out from under the covers to… "Wait. I don't have my phone with me. It's in the drawer in my room."

Pushing upright, Luke scanned the cabin. Eyes narrowed, he seemed to be homing in on the sound. Walking slowly across the small space, he cracked open the door enough to see into the hall and burst out laughing. "I love your grandmother."

As the words registered, she glanced at the ringing money belt in his hand.

"I'm guessing Sophia left this for you."

Retrieving the phone, she hit Call Return.

"*Helloo.*" Sophia sounded way too chipper.

"Good morning, Nana."

"Sorry I couldn't let you sleep in any longer. Heard from George. We're leaving for the island tour as soon as the ship clears customs. Herbie and I will meet you two at the breakfast buffet in twenty minutes. We'll catch you up then."

She looked at Luke and repeated *in twenty minutes* for his benefit.

He nodded, smiled that grin that was ever so slow to appear and way too potent to resist, and shrugged out of his shirt, flashing her an unexpected look at a fresh healing wound before closing the bathroom door behind him.

"Sharla?"

"Oh, sorry. See you in twenty, Nana."

She'd been a trauma nurse for too many years to kid herself into thinking a man could get a wound like that from an errant gardening tool. What had she allowed herself to step into? Even if she'd had any delusion that Luke's work was a glorified desk job, that glimpse of a recent wound on his side said otherwise. She'd promised herself *never again would she take a chance on a man with a dangerous job. Someone who put their life on the line every day.* And yet she was about to do exactly that. She didn't know whether to thank her grandmother or to kill her, but she could no more have walk away from him now than she could stop breathing.

Every scrap of common sense she had told her to steer clear. Not to let her heart get more involved. Except every fiber of her being screamed for her to spend every breathing moment of this trip right here entangled in his embrace. Oh, how she wanted to stay in his arms, bathed in that smile, listening to the sound of his voice hovering by her ear. But she had a terrible feeling that spending every day for the rest of the cruise in Luke's arms wouldn't be nearly long enough.

CHAPTER SEVENTEEN

"I'm sure this is a typical land fraud deal." Sophia speared a cantaloupe cube. "There are any number of ways he can run it, but my suspicion is the money is going to a bank account in the Caymans, and neither he nor anybody else buys an acre of property."

"You're probably right." Luke leaned closer over the table. He hadn't had time to share what he knew with Herbie last night or what Kate had texted him this morning. "My contact at my office says the land known as Miracle Bend is marshland owned and run by the Department of Agriculture. There actually are local government officials who want to sell the land. They've greased a lot of palms under the table and have come crazy close to pulling it off except for the surfers."

"The what?" Sharla asked.

"Surfers. They want to keep the waves pristine and natural. Distressed over the impending sale, one of them somehow came up with docs from an agreement with the township and the US government making the area a permanent wetland. Since the initial uproar, the Sierra Club and a long list of folks with lots of clout have gotten on the bandwagon. There is no way, no how, that this guy can sell you a single grain of sand from that acreage."

"That's what we suspected." Herbie set down his coffee cup and looked from Sharla to Luke to Sophia. "Sophia and I have had a bit of a disagreement over how to go about this."

"A bit," she clipped.

Herbie cut her a censuring glare filled with a heavy dose of love.

Before this cruise, before Sharla, Brooklyn never would have believed the strength of the connection the two older people had developed in such a short amount of time.

"Okay," Herbie continued, "we don't agree at all. But since this is my brother-in-law and my problem, we're going to do it my way. By the book."

Sophia rolled her eyes, blew out a sigh and grudgingly nodded.

Herbie kept his eye on her without saying a word until she repeated, "By the book."

"Let's get the skinny on this deal and catch the asshat." He dipped his chin at Sophia then Sharla. "Sorry for that, ladies."

"I've heard worse," Sophia answered at the same time Sharla said, "No problem."

"Then we're good to go?" Herbie asked.

All heads nodded in agreement. Herbie had a look of doubt that Luke suspected came from fear of what Sophia might pull out of her hat. Honestly Luke couldn't blame him. That lady was something else. But he was more concerned about the lost look on Sharla's face. They hadn't had time to discuss any of last night's surprises. Not sleeping curled in each other's arms, not his job and not her family's unique business history. Though, based on Sophia's brief explanation, he'd figured out Sharla was unlikely to have that much connection to the larcenous tendencies. It was no wonder she was less than sure of the whole plan. Not that what they had could be called a plan.

This was certainly not the navy's way of doing reconnaissance. It wasn't like SEALs to go in and just *see what happens*. He was used to having a boatload of intel and data before taking his men on a mission. But if he were going to be honest, even though this escapade was not the same as taking down terrorists, adrenaline was adrenaline, and bad guys were bad guys. Catching George Bailey at his own game was definitely going to be fun.

San Juan was a beautiful island. The ship docked in the old part of the city, affording the passengers an easy walk around the block to the narrow cobblestoned streets in search of restaurants and souvenirs.

"I hired a driver and a van." George stood by the yellow minivan cab. "It's a short drive out of town."

The drive was indeed not very long. They'd gone by crowded commercial areas and fashionable modern shopping malls.

But it was the pristine white beaches where the turtles nested that caught Sharla's eyes. "This is gorgeous."

"Yes." George beamed.

The driver pulled around to an open bay. Herbie was first out of the van, and he held his hand out for Gloria, then Nana. Luke exited next and did the same for Sharla.

When his fingers threaded with hers and didn't let go, she did her best to stay focused on the plan. What little there was of it. Slipping off her sandals, she followed the others onto the barren beach. In the distance to one side, a small mass of land jetted out with a blur of buildings perched atop.

"That's the Miramar Resorts and Hacienda. Built in 1985, it's the only resort within miles." George spun about to the other side of the road. "Farther that way toward the rain forest, there's a development of condos."

Sharla squinted into the sun. But there was nothing for her to see.

"And over here"—he faced away from the Miramar to a vast expanse of wavy grass with the occasional scattering of a cow or two—"this will be the spot." George rambled on about the land, the development, the plans, the cottages, the clubhouses.

Sharla didn't hear a word. All she could see was the pristine beauty of the area around her and the man still holding her hand.

"No wonder even the surfers care," she whispered to Luke.

He squeezed her hand. "It's nice to know this won't be covered with buildings and people by honest developers either."

While George and Gloria stood talking and gesturing with Herbie and her grandmother, Luke and Sharla veered off down the beach, walking along the water's edge.

"I love the ocean." She couldn't bring herself to look at him. Nearly alone on this beach, she didn't trust herself not to do or say something stupid.

"That's why you live in Miami."

"It's why I moved there, but I never make the time to go to the water. I guess it's a lot like native New Yorkers. No one actually goes to the Empire State Building or Times Square unless family comes for a visit."

"Makes sense."

They walked a few more feet, their pace slow, for here and now, everything felt good and comfortable. And right. She stole a glance in his direction. His gaze lingered on a distant point in the horizon. Where had he gone? What was he thinking? Did this new indefinable connection give her the right to know? And she wanted to know so many things about him. "Do you like living in Virginia?"

"It's just a house. Home is New York."

"Do you miss it?"

He flashed a half smile that made her forget about everything else except this place and time.

"Not so much the city, but my family. My mom and dad still live in the same house I grew up in. Our rooms haven't changed. My sisters' rooms are as pink and girly as they were when they were giddy teens. Same thing with my brother's and my room. Nothing's changed. My baseball and track trophies are where they've always been on the bookcase. Pennants from the Yankees cover one wall, and even my senior prom picture is proudly displayed."

His words brought a smile to her face. In only a few sentences she had a complete picture of who he'd been long ago. "Bet you looked good in a tux even then."

He tugged at his ear with his free hand and scrunched one side of his face. "I wouldn't take any bets on that if I were you. I don't think any seventeen-year-old boy looks good in a cummerbund."

"You may have a point. So all your siblings are still in

New York?"

"My sisters are. Mary, the oldest, is married with three kids. My middle sister, Abigail, much to my mother's chagrin, is still single. My brother, Steven, is in Florida."

"Really?"

"Yeah." He flashed that big smile. "Really. In Fort Lauderdale."

"Anyone in your family ever think about moving closer to your brother?" *Good grief.* Could she sound any pushier? She might as well have come right out and asked if he'd move to Florida for her. *Oh, Lord.* Why was she even letting her mind go there? "I mean—"

"Yeah. A lot actually." He drew to a stop and pinned her with a gaze so hot she was surprised not to have melted on the spot, "Especially lately."

"Yoo-hoo." Sophia jogged toward them, her grin as broad as the promenade aboard ship. "We're done visiting. George just happened to get a call from accounting as we stood there, and—surprise, surprise—there's room for two more investors. And here's the shocker. We have to move fast, or it will go to someone else."

Gathering her wits Sharla shifted gears, leaving worries about what to make of her new situation with Luke and concentrating on this mess her grandmother was getting into. "So now what?"

"We have lunch, go back to the ship and form a new plan."

"I'm telling you, we just have to run a con of our own. We can get this creep to cough up your brother-in-law's money." Sophia dropped onto the side of her bed. "There are at least a half-dozen cons we can pull off with only four people and a little ingenuity."

"No." Herbie sat down beside her. "You're not Robin Hood."

"Something simple. A shell game. Now you see it. Now

you don't."

"No," Herbie repeated.

Luke was staying out of the debate for now. He may not know how to run a confidence game, but he knew enough about working undercover and under the radar to know anything Sophia might have in mind would, at best, not be easy and, at worst, be downright deadly. Knowing it had been decades since Sophia had been involved in a real con meant preparing for the worst. But it was thoughts of Sharla caught up in the scheme that had his gut churning and his mind scrambling.

"We don't even know how many other people are involved," Herbie protested.

That seemed to give Sophia pause.

"For all we know"—Herbie grabbed Sophia's hand in his—"he could be a front man for the mob. And we don't need to run a con on the mob. Trust me on that."

Oh, how Luke wished his instincts weren't screaming FUBAR in the making.

"I'll admit"—Sophia covered their joined hands with her free hand—"he's not sharp enough to be running this on his own."

"These building plans don't look like anything drawn up on a do-it-yourself software program." Sharla sifted through the presentation packet George had left with Herbie and her grandmother. "Someone spent some money to have these designs made and then this portfolio put together. I'm with Herbie. He doesn't strike me as having this much skill."

"Agreed." Sophia pushed to her feet. "He's the charmer. The face. Someone else is the brains. Right now he's sitting back, thrilled that his game worked. Because it is a game to him. He played hard-to-get until he had us begging to give him our money. The adrenaline rush every grifter craves. No need to ask for money, the mark literally throws it at you. Whatever we do, we'll catch him by surprise. He thinks we're another couple of easy-to-snow senior citizens."

Sharla set the portfolio down on the table. "Can't we

just show this to the police and let them take it from here? I'm sure if I called Tyler, he could get the right people involved."

"Any law enforcement agency—and DA—is going to want more than our word that he's a crook." Herbie reached for Sophia's hand and tugged her back to the space next to him.

Sharla pointed to the papers on the table. "We have these designs, and we know who actually owns the land."

Herbie shook his head. "Not a single thing in those papers shows the legal description of the land they tried to sell us today. We have nothing to give the authorities."

Luke already knew what needed to happen, and, no matter how Herbie chose to proceed, Luke would make sure Sharla stayed as far away from this caper as he could keep her. "So what do you propose?"

"We play along. Agree to his deal. Make him as comfortable as a pig in a sty. When we exchange the cash for whatever phony documentation he provides with legal property descriptions and the sham corporation info, we'll have the evidence, and the authorities will have caught him red-handed."

Sophia eyed Herbie skeptically. "What authorities?"

"Yeah, well…" Herbie ran his hand along the back of his neck. "That depends on where all of this comes down. If we can stall till we dock back home, I can probably get the ball rolling."

"Not likely," Sophia said. "There's more to this con, and it plays out in St. Thomas. According to George that's where their Caribbean offices are, and, if you and I want in, we have to have the cash before we leave St. Thomas."

Taking George down in St. Thomas was the first thing Luke had heard this afternoon that didn't make his gut roil. "Better for us. If there really is an office and any other people involved, St. Thomas will be the place to nab them. With the land deal and the money exchange both being in US territories, this falls to one agency, the FBI."

Herbie's spine stiffened. "That will be a little tougher. In my day, cops dealing with the Feds usually meant a pissing match."

"And what about the cash?" Sophia asked. "I don't have that kind of money."

Luke shrugged. "No problem. I'll handle everything."

All heads snapped in his direction.

If this was going to happen, there was no way he was leaving the details to anyone else. Especially not if he wanted to keep Sharla and Sophia out of harm's way. "I'll make the calls. Get the authorities on board. We just need to nail down the place and make sure George has the right paperwork with him when the exchange happens so the arrest sticks."

Even though US agencies like the CIA and FBI were famous for not playing nice or sharing information, most agents were always willing to return a favor. Especially when your intel brought down a terrorist-funding plot in Small Town, USA, long before all hell could break loose in the media. Luke still had the phone numbers.

"So that's it?" Sophia sprang up, fisted hands landing on her hips. "We're just going to turn these guys over and not recover any of the stolen money swindled from your brother-in-law?"

"The Feds will confiscate their belongings and recover whatever money they can. There will be some compensation." Herbie's voice came out tired and raspy and not very reassuring.

Sitting back down, Sophia muttered, "We all know how well that worked out for Bernie Madoff's investors."

The next thirty minutes were spent hammering out the details. It was in essence very simple. Herbie and Sophia would arrive at a designated location with fifty thousand US dollars and not relinquish the money until Good Old George turned over the incriminating phony investment paperwork. All Luke would have to do—in the next few days before they docked in St. Thomas—was convince the FBI to get involved, make sure the local authorities did their part, and, oh, yeah, get his hands on fifty thousand dollars to use as bait.

CHAPTER EIGHTEEN

"Yes." Sophia leaned forward and scribbled "Lady Madonna" on the piece of paper.

Gloria gave a quick thumbs-up, then slapped Sophia with a high-five. Over the last three days and three island ports, the two had become friendlier than a sniper and his rifle. And that made Luke just a wee bit nervous.

The next tune played, and the bridge of Sophia's nose crinkled in thought. When the cruise staff played the beginning notes of the song a second time, Sophia spun around to Gloria only to find the same pensive glare staring back at her.

Suddenly Gloria's eyes opened wide, and she hurriedly scrawled something on her scratch paper before passing it over to Sophia. The fired-up redhead slapped another high-five at Sophia, and Luke had to sip his drink to stifle a laugh.

"You know"–Sharla leaned in and set her hand on his–"Mom says Nana was the only grown woman she knew who cried the day it was announced the Beatles had broken up."

"Can't see it." He folded his fingers around hers. Ever since the day in San Juan, they'd done a considerable bit of hand-holding and he'd done his best to control the heady kisses, and everyone was on their best behavior, preparing for the big day.

Which helped him keep his focus. Especially since he only had the rest of the cruise to convince Sharla that he was more than his job. On Tortola, they laughed over Sharla's great-aunts' crazy antics while she helped Luke pick out gifts for his family. Touring the grounds of the old fort in St. Kitts, they discovered a mutual interest in history. And by yesterday, relaxing over food and drinks from a beachfront balcony in St. Maarten, Luke had felt as though Sharla had always been at his side. Imagining himself back to his lone-wolf way of life seemed impossible. He had no choice; he had to win her heart.

Except tonight his mind was on other concerns, like Sharla's growing anxiety. While Sophia seemed to be having the time of her life, and Herbie appeared completely nonplussed about tomorrow's big takedown, Sharla looked like a soft wind would be enough to have her jumping out of her skin.

"And the title for song number three?" Becky asked into the mic.

"Lady Madonna," Gloria and Sophia echoed.

The routine continued down the line. Song after song, they cheered, laughed, bumped fists and overall acted like a couple of college kids on spring break. Even the ladies in the red hats got in on the minifestivities. By the time Becky got to song number fifteen, the Red Hats had shifted their chairs closer. By number twenty, all the women were singing and toasting each correct answer.

Tapping her fingers on her lap, Sharla merely smiled stiffly and sipped her strawberry daiquiri.

This evening's grand prizes for the winning team members were picture frame magnets. Probably the most useful of the awards for anyone who liked to stick papers to their fridge. Luke would give his to his mother. She'd like that.

Sophia stood up, a pomegranate martini in her hand and her spoils in the other. "Okay, where to now?"

"The dance party. You coming?" Wide-Brimmed Red Hat Lady was swinging her hips in place to the Beatles tunes still playing overhead.

"That's right." Sophia linked elbows with Red Hat Lady. "We'll show these kids how it's done."

"Absolutely," four women in red hats echoed.

Drinks in hand and Gloria in tow, the group of laughing ladies wandered off, leaving Herbie and George standing alone.

"Casino?" Herbie asked.

"Casino," George agreed.

"You two joining us or the cackling hens?" Herbie asked almost as a second thought.

"I think we'll take a walk." Luke hadn't asked Sharla what she'd prefer to do, but he'd already decided she needed to get away from the Baileys, and fresh air would be just the medicine the doctor ordered. Or the next best thing.

"Thank you."

Sharla linked arms with him, and his heart swelled at the progress they'd made the last few days. For one thing, she wasn't blushing anymore every time she looked at him.

"I really do like walking out here at night. It's so peaceful, and the stars are magnificent."

"Not much competition for sparkle in the middle of the ocean." He let his hand slide down and thread with hers.

"No. No, there isn't." They walked an entire lap in silence. Another lap later, Sharla blew out a sigh. "Nana seems to think all this is one big game."

"I'm not surprised. From the stories she'd told the last couple of days, some of those cons would make great movies. The one where she and her sisters had to sell Daddy's farm before the bank foreclosed. To four different people. And they didn't even own the place."

"And they only had a few days while the family who did own the property was on vacation."

"It sounded like they should all have won Academy Awards."

"Nana always said you can't con an honest man. She was so proud of the fact that they only took those who had already taken others."

"You believe that?"

"Yeah. I think I do." Sharla led him off the path and over to the railing. Standing beside him, she studied the moon hanging low in the distance. "I also think this is like a walk down memory lane for her. And it scares me."

"I won't let anything happen to her." He tipped his head and placed a lightly there kiss on her temple. "I think she knows what she's doing. She's certainly put her all into getting friendly with Gloria."

"She's been working overtime to make sure they don't think she or Herbie are suspicious."

"And she's doing a bang-up job."

"Yeah." Pivoting slightly, she tilted her head to watch him. "So are you."

"Me?"

"Getting all the right people involved. Arranging for the money. That's above and beyond the call of duty, and awfully nice of you."

"I'm glad I could help." He honestly was afraid that, if he didn't help Herbie nab this guy, Sophia would have called every relative under the sun to put together a sweet, complicated and dangerous con. "The money will be waiting for them at the St. Thomas National Bank. This way, if George or Gloria wants to tag along, the entire transaction will look legit. It will seem as though Sophia's and Herbie's banks in Florida had wired the money."

"What if he insists we meet his partner at their office?"

Luke doubted George would want that. Luke doubted the crook even had an office. He wasn't even all that sure there was an accomplice. He expected George to collect the money and make a beeline to the nearest branch of the Cayman Island Bank. Funds never to be traced again.

"I wouldn't worry about it. We stick to the plan. You and I will go with them. Then before the transactions take place, we'll bid our good-byes to go shopping. You'll go on ahead, and I'll keep an eye on them. When it's all over, I'll call you."

"I said it before, and I'll say it again. I don't like that part."

"It will be okay." He kissed her forehead again.

Her eyes fluttered shut. "I can't think when you do that."

"Don't think." The temptation to dip his chin and press his lips to hers was fighting a losing battle with his carefully timed plan to win her trust and then her heart. Only then would he be able to make her see past what he did for a living. He hoped.

"Could you do that again?"

Her hand slid up his chest and cast the final blow in his inner battle. His mouth covering hers, all the sensations that had swarmed him the other night took over. He could kiss her all night, every night, forever. When her hands strolled higher and hooked around his neck, his mouth lingered moments longer before he found the strength to pull back. "You really are a great kisser."

"You're no slouch."

His forehead resting against hers, he closed his eyes and tried to put his thoughts into perspective. Form words that made sense. He couldn't keep this up for much longer. Time to test the waters. "I've been thinking about visiting my brother in Fort Lauderdale with the rest of my vacation time."

"Really?" She kept her arms wound around his neck.

He didn't move. "Don't know of a SEAL who isn't fond of water."

A shallow breath blew in his face, and she pulled away, sending his heart sinking to the pit of his stomach. "What about CIA *employees*? Do they like the water too?"

His job. Though to him the CIA was only that, a job. A duty. Not who he was. There was no way to explain, without pushing her away further, how, even if he never again served in Uncle Sam's Navy, deep in his soul, he would always be a SEAL. "I've trained all of my adult life to serve."

Taking another step back, her chin dipped once, and her mouth tilted upward in a shaky smile. "I know. Danny was the same way. It's what you do."

And just like that she turned to the yellow path, walked out of the wind, into the hall, and away from him.

CHAPTER NINETEEN

"How can you stay so calm?" Sharla twirled her hair into a bun at the back of her head for the third time this morning and stabbed it with another bobby pin.

"Sweetie, this is too easy. We're not the ones orchestrating a con. We're just turning up to watch the show."

Sharla's shaky fingers reached for another pin, and, just as had happened before, she'd missed the mark, and the heavy knot slipped to one side.

"Oh, for heaven's sake. You're not going to Cinderella's ball." Sophia grabbed a scrunchie off the vanity desk, handed it to Sharla and then patted her on the shoulder. "Everything will be fine. You'll be fine. And I like your hair in a ponytail."

"Thanks, Nana." Maybe she was right. Maybe Sharla was overstressing. Herbie had been a cop for forty years, and he didn't seem at all concerned about the upcoming rendezvous. Yeah. She could do this. A rap on the door sounded, and she dropped the brush, springing to her feet.

"Come on in, guys." Sophia opened the door. "I think we need to get Sharla a drink before we go anywhere."

Luke and Herbie turned to her. Herbie was frowning, but Luke simply eyed her with an intense scrutiny that made her insides go on high alert, and had her mind forgettimg all about cons and swindles and traps.

"Maybe you should stay here," Herbie suggested.

"Nonsense." Sophia kissed her granddaughter's cheek and patted her shoulder again. "She'll be fine once she sees how easy this is going to be. Though a mimosa may not be a bad idea. Just to take the edge off."

There was no way Sharla would stay on the ship while her grandmother was off baiting crooks. Plastering on a smile that she hoped looked confident and not terrified, she nodded and linked arms with the former grifter. "Nana's right. I'll be fine. And I don't need a drink. Let's just get this show on the road!"

"You sure, honey?" Herbie asked, his frown still in place.

She smiled in earnest. Not that she was any more certain, but the sincerity of his concern touched her.

"Okay then. George confirmed he and Gloria will meet us at the coffee shop across the street from the bank."

"And I've already touched base with my contact. Money's in place and ready to go. Looks like we're all set." Luke held out his hand to Sharla. "As you said, time to get this show on the road."

With more eagerness than she would have liked, she accepted the proffered arm, and followed the others out the door and down the hall. As much as she hated to admit it, having Luke to hold on to did more to calm her nerves than a vat of mimosas. And why was that? She'd known this man little more than a week. Why did having him near make everything in her world seem so right? Even when that world was in a state of complete and total batshit-crazy.

In the elevator Luke leaned closer and whispered, "What's the matter?"

"You're kidding me right?"

"No, I mean, you're staring at me."

"Oh. I... wasn't staring." Right and moths don't like flames. Was that what she was? A moth attracted to the deadly flame.

"Color me surprised," Sophia muttered as the elevator doors opened.

Snapped out of her self-analysis, Sharla glanced in the direction her grandmother seemed to be looking. George and Gloria stood near the end of the disembarkation line.

"Showtime." Sophia's face lit up with a bright smile, and she stepped off the elevator laughing. Whether that was for the Baileys' benefit or simply the thrill of the game, Sharla didn't know. But following her grandmother's example, she relaxed her shoulders, threaded her hand with Luke's and laughed delightfully at something he hadn't said. Nana looked back over her shoulder at Sharla and winked. A fun, sparkly wink.

Maybe she could do this after all.

"Oh, hi." Gloria waved at the group as though accidentally running into each other hadn't been their plan all along.

Though truthfully, had it not been for Nana's comment on spotting them, Sharla would have believed bumping into them was simply coincidence. Or perhaps Providence. And most likely so would their other marks. The idea of all the senior citizens who these con artists had swindled out of their much-needed savings had Sharla's blood pumping fast, hard and furious through her veins.

Her head had always understood the situation, but only now did it seem all too real. And like her grandmother, she was ready to take these suckers *down*.

"We were going to go straight to the café and have a little snack. We might as well walk together." George raised an arm and waved for the group to get in front of him in line. As each person in line departed, the repetitive *ding* from the keycards grew louder until the six of them were off the ship and chatting away.

Gloria paused at one of the portside duty-free shops, and Sophia abandoned Herbie and sidled up beside Gloria, the two oohing and aahing over this bauble and that. Like generations of dinner parties, within minutes, the women and men had migrated to be with their own kind. In this case the men leading the way talking sports and politics, and the women lagging behind pausing at whatever storefront caught their eye, laughing and joking all the way.

Well, Gloria and Sophia were doing most of the bonding.

Sharla seemed to be along just for the ride. A small part of her was fascinated watching her grandmother and wished she could have been a fly on the wall back in the day to see the family pull off a long con.

"We'll see you in a few." At the bank door, George waved to them and walked away with his wife.

"I would have thought they'd come in with us." Sharla crossed the threshold behind her grandmother.

"That would have been too pushy," Luke whispered to her. "Notice neither mentioned anything about the deal or the money while we walked over. They simply wanted to make sure we didn't develop last-minute cold feet. I'd bet all the money that someone here is watching us for them."

Sharla almost turned her head to study the surrounding faces when Luke leaned into her again. "Don't look."

So a con artist she wasn't meant to be. But what did it say about Luke that he knew how to do this? Knew not to look? And knew she was about to? He said it himself; deep in his soul, he was a SEAL. The military's most elite warriors. Though his team most likely never robbed banks, she had no doubt they could have infiltrated the building, gathered up all the money and valuables, and been long gone before anyone was the wiser. Isn't that what they did in foreign lands with valuable information or people? Save the captured. Destroy the weapons used against Americans. Along with so many other things ordinary citizens would never know of. She would never know of. But he didn't do that anymore. Or did he?

Both Sophia and Herbie sat with the bank manager, signed a long list of papers and received a lecture from the man on the perils of walking through the city with that much cash. Herbie assured the nervous man that they would be fine but neglected to mention he was a retired policeman. Something Sharla had noticed hadn't been mentioned to anyone else during the cruise.

Through the bank window she could see George and Gloria sitting chatting at the café across the street. Which meant, in a couple of hours, this would all be behind them. After the conversation last night, being reminded that Luke and Danny had been trained to serve, she realized she couldn't do this again. Couldn't lay her heart on the line with a man who could die any minute doing his job. Logic told her that anybody could die at any minute. Every day, people were killed in accidents, diagnosed with terminal diseases or simply dropped dead on the street like her grandpa. But she'd bought into that logic before, and she just couldn't take the chance again. She just couldn't.

When the bank manager walked away, leaving Herbie and Nana alone in the vault to count and sign for the cash in private, Luke nudged her. "You have that look of a scared rabbit in your eyes again. Are you going to be okay? Should I ask for a glass of water?"

How did he do that? How did he know what she was feeling just by looking in her eyes? And what was she supposed to do about the way her heart beat slightly faster every time he did? For that matter, how was she supposed to stay away from him—for the rest of her life?

"We're all set." Sophia clutched her shoulder bag. "On we go."

So far everything was going exactly as Luke had predicted. The bank manager did his carefully rehearsed speech like a pro. Working with Sophia was a plus. The woman knew how to play a part and play it well. Not a single person would suspect she carried fifty thousand in cash.

They hadn't made it fully across the street when George and Gloria stood to greet them. Alone. Maybe there wasn't an accomplice. He'd had Kate searching data banks every day for known associates, but she'd not come up with anyone who could be here now.

George stuck out his hand first. "Just a few more minutes until our local associate arrives with the paperwork, and you'll be wealthy real estate investors."

Sophia smiled, not as brightly as before, and raised her hand gently to her temple. "Yes. Isn't it exciting?"

Herbie eyed Sophia carefully, then shot Luke a questioning glance.

All Luke could do was blink. He couldn't afford to offer even the slightest tell of not knowing what that was all about.

Inside, the café was more crowded than Luke would have liked. Patrons scattered here and there at different tables. A few he recognized from the ship, including Frenchy, the second officer from the fire incident.

The six of them maneuvered around a table in the back corner. Luke vying with Herbie and George for the seat along the wall. Since the plan was for Luke and Sharla to leave before the transactions went down, he let Herbie have the prime seat. George sat beside him.

"You know"—Sophia rubbed the corners of her eyes—"I'm not feeling very well. I think I forgot to take my blood pressure medicine."

George's eyes rounded, but Gloria stood quickly to step over and place her arm around Sophia's shoulder, nearly colliding with Sharla who had done the same thing.

Sophia put up her hand. "I'm okay. Just a little dizzy. Some blurry vision. I'm sure it's the stupid meds." She turned to Sharla. "Honey, I'd better go back to the ship. You have the money. Herbie will be here. You go ahead and sign for me."

"I'm afraid that won't be possible." George cleared his throat. "Unless she has power of attorney."

"Oh, dear." Sophia rubbed at her temple some more, considering her options. "I hate to miss this opportunity, but I really need to get back to the ship. Let's do this. Just put my granddaughter's name on the paperwork. She'll initial the changes and sign. The deal will be hers."

"Nana?"

"Honey, it's okay. You'd inherit it anyway. And I know you won't cheat me out of my earnings while I'm alive."

Gloria had the good grace to drop her eyes at the comment.

George showed no signs of guilt. Jerk.

"Nana, I can't—"

"It's okay, honey. Herbie's here." Sophia turned to

Luke. "Handsome, I think I could use an escort back to the ship."

Crap. Was this for real or did Sophia have something up her sleeve? Something neither him nor Herbie were going to like. Holding back a sigh, he had to consider his options quickly. Herbie had to stay for sure or the whole thing would go down the drain, and Luke's chances of pulling all these strings again, if nothing came of this today, would be slim to none. With *none* taking the lead. Which meant doing as Sophia suggested, and leaving Sharla with Herbie and the Baileys.

He didn't like that one bit. Herbie had been a cop—according to Kate a helluva good one—but he wasn't armed, which would make protecting Sharla much harder if this deal didn't go down as choreographed. He had no choice. *Blast.*

"I'll be back when I'm sure she's okay." He looked to Sharla, surprised she didn't look more panicked. Even more surprised to see determination in her eyes. *Attagirl.* Just don't do anything stupid. *Please.*

Offering Sophia his arm, the lady accepted gladly and shuffled her way outside. When they'd made it to the ship's gangway, she turned and patted him on the arm. "I'm okay from here. I'll grab a crew member inside to escort me to the cabin for my meds. The doctor will be a phone call away if I need him. You go do your thing as planned."

He loved this old lady. In only a week, he'd come to love her almost as much as her granddaughter. If anything happened to Sophia, he'd never forgive himself. Nor would Sharla. But if anything happened to Sharla,... God, he didn't even want to go there. No wonder she didn't want any part of a man whose life was on the line every day.

"Go." Sophia nudged him. "Don't you let anything happen to my little girl."

"I won't." He took a step back, then another. "Don't make me regret this."

"I'll be fine. Just get those crooks," she said more steadily.

With that final reassurance, Luke turned and wove

through the crowd to the back streets, making his way to his predetermined location. Out of sight from the café's patrons, the rooftop across the way had everything he needed waiting for him. Gotta love connections.

CHAPTER TWENTY

All Sharla wanted was to turn over this money to the creeps and get back to her grandmother. At this point she almost didn't care if they were caught or not. Almost.

"I certainly hope she's all right." Gloria shook her head. "She's such a nice lady."

Herbie had kept his gaze focused on the window long after Nana and Luke had disappeared from view.

The man was too quiet. His concern for her grandmother helped make Sharla feel better. The way things looked, once this was all over, he and Nana were going to be an item for sure. Sharla wouldn't be surprised if she lost her roommate.

"Here he is." George stood and waved a slim middle-aged man in a Panama hat over to the table.

"How do you do?" Extending his hand to Herbie, the man offered a brief smile.

"Herbie Klein."

"Sharla Kramer."

Casting a furtive glance around the room, Mr. Panama Hat took a seat, at no time volunteering his name. "Shall we get started?" He set down a leather briefcase that most likely cost more money than Sharla earned in a week and pulled out a stack of papers.

"There's been a slight change of plans," George announced.

"Oh." The associate raised a brow in question, once again quickly scanning the café before settling his attention back on George.

"Ms. Garibaldi took ill. Miss Kramer will be purchasing

the shares for her grandmother."

"Hmm. County Records frown on handwritten changes to transfer documents."

"I know," Gloria said. "But she's such a nice lady. Don't you think this once…"

The associate shifted his focus from her to George. George barely bobbed his chin, but that seemed to be all the reassurance Panama Hat needed. "All right. Let's get these out."

Sharla crossed out Nana's name, printed her own, then initialed the change and handed it to George for his initials. Herbie gave the papers a cursory glance, though Sharla knew he was looking for one thing. The incriminating legal description of the land the con artists had no right to sell. She knew he'd found it when he nodded and flipped more quickly through the remaining pages.

Holding the bag of money in her lap, tightly secured with one hand, Sharla shifted every time someone walked by. Herbie was the first to sign the pile of papers. Mr. Panama Hat stamped each page with what she assumed to be some sort of notarizing authority. Normally she would have asked, but, since she already knew the deal wasn't legit, what was the point.

According to the original plan, Luke was supposed to be watching from somewhere. Knowing he was nearby gave her an unexpected sense of calm. She could only hope that her grandmother hadn't needed him to stay with her. At this point she didn't know what had her more unsettled: this crazy scheme they'd gotten involved in, not being sure if Luke was nearby as planned or wondering how Nana was doing.

Sophia exited the elevator and turned down the hall. Walking past an older couple moving slower than molasses in winter, she waited for them to turn the corner before sliding on the pair of gloves she'd pilfered from the medical center downstairs and stopped at 720. A suite. *Of course.* Pulling the keycard from her pocket, she slid it into the door, pushed down the handle and shoved the door open.

"And we're in." She loved it when a plan came together. Taking the card had been a last-minute impulse, but, as her daddy always said, when Providence hands you an opportunity, grab it with both hands. She glanced around the cabin. Somewhere in here there had to be information she could use to help recoup the fifty thousand dollars taken from Herbie's brother-in-law. Everyone else was welcome to sit back and let the Feds handle restitution. Not Sophia Garibaldi.

"Wish you could be here, Benny. This is a fun one. Did you notice the way I got the card? Dumb woman was so busy playing happy tourist at every shop window to keep me from skipping out on them, she never noticed when I lifted the pouch with the keycard. Really dumb."

Not really expecting to find anything in the drawers, handbags or stowed luggage, Sophia went after the cabinet safe. Digital was a bit more challenging but not impossible. She tried the first code she'd settled on. Nothing. Then the next and another. So maybe George was a little smarter than Sophia had given him credit for. Shuffling through the data in her mind that Luke had shown them on the two hustlers, Sophia tried all the possible codes for George and moved on to Gloria. Three tries later Sophia hit pay dirt with the date when the flashy redhead had graduated high school. *Interesting.*

Inside, right on top, a couple thousand in cash. Not what she would have expected from a guy playing high roller. But it was something the Feds could confiscate now. Under the money she found bank deposit slips. "Well, this is more like it." No wonder he didn't have a lot of cash on him. One slip came from the First National Bank of the Netherland Antilles, St. Maarten. The ship's most recent stop. A deposit of twenty-five thousand. Chump change. Available balance. *Bingo.* Over three-quarters of a million dollars. Resisting the urge to do a happy dance, she put the receipt on the table and snapped a couple of photos. If the Feds didn't follow through on this, she knew some people who could. She took two more snapshots, careful to zoom in on the account numbers and the names on each. "I'll be damned."

Returning her attention to the safe, she lifted a stack of passports. *Oh, what fun.* Passports for Antonio and Gloria Montanaccio. *Interesting.* Passports for George and Gloria Bailey. British passports for Archibald and Thelma Brisbane. *Very interesting.* Underneath everything, a faded manila envelope the size of a half sheet of paper was the last thing in the small safe. Carefully she opened the lip and let the contents slide onto the counter. Staring at the folded pieces of colorful paper, it took her a few minutes to piece together that she'd just discovered the mother lode. Five-thousand-dollar bearer bonds issued in 1978. *What kind of nut carries these things around on vacation?* Counting quickly she came up with fifteen bonds totaling seventy-five thousand dollars. Her cheeks tugged upward in a tight grin. "Imagine that."

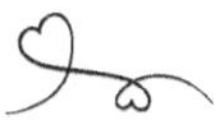

Still worried about her grandmother, Sharla set her phone on the table and hoped someone would call or text her soon that Nana was all right. She'd signed the first two pages when the phone rang.

"Excuse me," she said to Mr. Panama Hat who looked none too happy at the interruption. As a matter of fact the deep-set creases between his bushy brows made his gaze look downright menacing. "Hello?… Oh, Nana.… Mmm-hmm… Mmm-hmm… Yes.… Okay. I love you too."

"How is she?" Gloria asked.

"In our room, lying down and feeling much better."

"Good. So glad to hear it."

The associate tapped his finger on the next page, and Sharla resumed her signing.

Nana had apologized for leaving her alone and gave her a quick reminder of Nana's part in the plan. Nana was supposed to let the authorities know the transaction was complete by tugging on her ear. When Sharla signed the last page, she dropped the pen on the page and tugged. Waited. And nothing.

Something wasn't right. Weren't the good guys supposed to swoop in now and save the day? As casually as she could she glanced around the café, searching the faces of the patrons, the waiter, the cashier, wondering if any had the face of the local police or FBI.

"Miss." The man tapped the table again. "If you will discreetly hand me the bag, we'll verify the funds."

Oh, brother. In her anxiousness to be done, she hadn't realized she was still clutching the beach bag stuffed with more money than she'd probably ever see in one place in her lifetime.

"Yes." George grinned at her. "Then you'll be on the ground floor of one of the biggest new development projects San Juan has seen in decades."

Sliding the bag across the table, Sharla looked around again and tugged at her ear.

"Are your ears bothering you, honey? I have some drops I use when I travel. You never know what's going to hit you in a strange place." Gloria dug through her purse, paused, frowned and began removing things one by one, placing them on the table.

"What are you doing?" George asked.

"My ship's pouch is gone."

George leaned over her shoulder and looked at the empty bag.

"My key pass is in there. I can't get back on the ship without it."

"Or into the room," George added, turning to Herbie and Sharla.

Once again Sharla reached for her ear. Before she could tug, the sound of a chair scraping against the tile floor struck her at the same time the pressure of a strong weight crushed her throat.

"It's a setup." In a single move, Mr. Panama Hat had slung the bag of money over his shoulder and pulled Sharla hard against him. One arm strangling her against him, the other held a gun to her temple.

Oh, God.

"She doesn't have an earache," the gunman growled, "she's signaling someone."

The sound of a woman's scream blended with more chairs scraping and shoes tapping hurriedly on the floor. The cashier stood but didn't move. The waiter shoved the screaming lady and her husband behind an overturned table.

"Al," George said in a huff, "are you crazy?"

"Tell me where's Gloria's keycard?"

"Some kid picked her pocket." For the first time, George looked truly panicked. Color drained from his cheeks and beads of sweat appeared along his hairline. "Seriously, man."

"George. No one's been near me except..." Gloria looked around before her gaze settled coldly on Sharla.

"I'm sure this is all a big misunderstanding." Herbie raised his hands, palms open, to the man squeezing Sharla's throat more tightly.

Stars began to play in front of her eyes. She clutched at his arm trying to pull it free. Somewhere in the back of her mind, all the self-protection rules Danny had taught her slowly unfolded. At the awkward angle Mr. Panama Hat held her, she didn't dare try any of them. Not without fear he'd shoot someone else. If only she could get her foot closer to his.

"Take it easy. The young lady can't breathe." Clearly enunciated in a low, calming tone, Herbie sounded like one of those negotiators on TV.

She only hoped he was as good.

"Why don't you let her go, and we'll talk."

Gloria eased backward, closer to the door. George seemed to be contemplating the same, when Mr. Panama Hat shifted his weight and turned slightly. "No one goes anywhere."

Herbie tried again to reason with the guy, but his grip on Sharla's throat didn't ease up.

When Gloria took another step backward, Mr. Panama yelled, "One more move and I'll shoot."

The cool feel of the metal against her temple gave way to a faint blow of warm air as his arm flung straight out, pointing the gun at Gloria. This was Sharla's chance. Hoping the trick worked as well in sandals as in high heels, she slammed her heel down hard onto Mr. Panama's instep.

A loud crack ripped through the small café. That same woman let out another scream. The weight on Sharla's neck fell away. The waiter bolted to the door, grabbing Gloria. The cashier hurtled over the counter, tackling George. And Mr. Panama Hat lay dead on the floor. A bullet hole between his eyes.

From his rooftop perch Luke had had a clear shot aimed at George's alleged partner. The last barrier between nabbing the cons and enjoying the rest of his vacation with Sharla. He'd noticed the way the character had started eyeing her. Fidgeting more as she played with her phone. Each time she tugged on her ear, the guy grew increasingly agitated. Luke had come within seconds of breaking his position to call and tell her to stop that.

The agent posted on the corner overrode her signal when he got closer to the door and saw the money still hadn't changed hands. Luke's contacts inside the café couldn't budge until the local authorities moved. And then the sleazebag did the last stupid thing in his life: he used Sharla for a human shield.

Luke would gladly shoot him down again if he could.

The rifle still in his hand, he bolted down the stairs and across the empty street, every second thanking God that Sharla wasn't the one with a bullet in her head. Rushing through the open doorway, he stopped at the first face he recognized and handed off the weapon. "Thanks, man."

"Glad I came. Didn't expect this."

"We never do." Not really listening to what his friend was saying, Luke scanned the room quickly.

The locals had George and Gloria in handcuffs. Gloria

was spitting and snarling as she and George were escorted off the premises. Frenchy and another man Luke didn't recognize were already rendering aid, assisting frightened patrons out from their hiding spots behind tables and counters, and gathering the ship's passengers to one side.

In the opposite corner from where they'd sat signing papers, Sharla stood curled in Herbie's arms.

Whatever his FBI friend was still saying to him didn't register. "Excuse me." Luke needed to get across the room. Now.

"I called her grandmother." Herbie let his arm fall away from around Sharla. "Sophia should be here any second."

Luke reached around and tugged Sharla against him. No triumph in the field had ever left him as elated as the moment when Sharla was free from the crook with a gun. And even that paled in comparison to having her in his arms now. "I'm sorry."

"I can't believe it." She leaned into him.

Neither could he. The idea of what would have happened to her, of what else could have gone wrong—if his FBI contact hadn't come himself with two of his best guys or hadn't arranged a rifle for Luke—made his blood pressure soar. Even now, holding her safely in his arms, his heart still pounded furiously against his ribs. He could have lost her.

The ship's officer Luke didn't recognize sat at a table with the handful of passengers from the ship and a local policeman. Crime scene guys and more officers from the ship filed in. Frenchy came and stood beside Herbie.

"I regret this unfortunate incident." Frenchy turned to face Sharla. "But I see you are in good hands. If there is anything we can do to be of assistance..." He let his words hang.

Sharla gave a halfhearted nod.

"Thank God." Arms open wide, Sophia came hurrying in, wrapping herself around her granddaughter and Luke. "I knew George and Gloria weren't a problem. I should have stuck around to check out the other guy. I'm so sorry, honey."

For a long while no one moved. Finally Sophia stepped back to face Luke. "Tell your friends, when they interrogate those two, that Gloria's either the brains or sticking it to Good Old George."

And how the hell did she know that?

"Don't look at me that way."

"Nana. You didn't."

"Had I known you were going to be in danger, baby, I wouldn't have."

"Oh, Nana."

Luke stepped aside and let the two women love on each other.

Lagging behind as the passengers and his fellow officers made their way to the front door, Frenchy turned and moved next to Luke. "I see you're still playing hero."

Though spoken with the same even tone as after the fire incident earlier on the cruise, this time, to Luke, the words rang cold and sharp. He barely shook his head.

"Once again"—Frenchy gave a single dip of his chin. The slightest of nods—"thank you, Lieutenant." Then walked away.

The deference to Luke's rank gave him no pleasure. This was no game. Not the kind he wanted to play. Not anymore. Silently watching Sophia and Sharla apologize to each other for everything from not understanding to not thinking, Luke made some fast choices.

"You done good." Herbie moved beside him, legs apart at parade rest, arms crossed.

Luke didn't say anything.

"You know, there are more people like us. Everywhere."

This time Luke dragged his gaze away from the woman he knew beyond a doubt he didn't want to live without to look at Herbie. "Us?"

"Well, not exactly us. But people getting taken in one way or another. Some by professionals, some by spouses, businessmen, even their children."

He'd been thinking almost the exact same thing. Bad guys were bad guys. And with the right people, he could help a lot of the good guys without putting his life on the line every day. "Yeah," he agreed. "There are. You want in?"

The ends of Herbie's mouth curled up in a Cheshire grin.

Apparently Luke wasn't the only one ready for a change. All he had to do now was sell the idea to Sharla.

CHAPTER TWENTY-ONE

Federal agents and local port authorities were all over the Baileys' cabin like ants on sugar. Earlier Luke had stood by Sharla while his FBI buddy had questioned her and her grandmother. Very thankful to the guy for keeping it short and sweet, and for agreeing to wait until after they returned to port stateside to obtain any additional information from the family. After all they both knew nothing from here on would be done quickly.

Once on board, Herbie hadn't wanted to leave Sophia's side, and neither Sophia nor Luke had wanted to relinquish custody of Sharla. In the end, the four wound up on the promenade deck, leaning against the railing, an adult beverage in hand, watching the agents leave the ship with the Baileys' belongings.

Making a tsk-tsk sound, Sophia slowly shook her head. "What are the odds in the few hours they had to process their room that the chain of evidence didn't get totally screwed up?"

"You don't know that," Herbie said.

"We'll see. In the meantime, good thing I got these." Sophia pulled out her phone and looked to Luke. "I should have thought to send you this earlier, but, when I heard about Sharla, everything else slipped away. Give me your cell number."

In only a few seconds, photos of passports, along with bank deposit slips in the name of Gloria Montanaccio and Thelma Brisbane popped up in his in-box. No wonder Antonio had failed at everything until he became George Bailey. If Gloria had control of all the money, she probably had control of everything else too. Or, as Sophia had said earlier, was setting up Good Old George for the fleecing of his life.

Sophia pointed at her phone. "Maybe you can use some of your connections to make sure the money in those bank accounts doesn't disappear."

Without a word Luke immediately forwarded the data to Kate. If there was any way to jump the gun on freezing funds, she'd know how to do it. Sophia had done good. He had to admire the old broad, even if she had put her granddaughter at risk. Sharla simply didn't have the instincts to make a good con artist.

Luke put away his phone and took a sip of his bourbon. Over the rim of the glass, his gaze remained level with Sophia. "Do I even want to know how you got into her room?"

Sophia shrugged. "I'd noticed where Gloria put the card after we left the ship. Had several chances. But the perfume parlor was irresistible. She'd leaned forward on the counter shoving her bag out of the way. Even an apprentice could have lifted the thing undetected."

"I can see we're going to have to have a long talk about your skill sets." Herbie's words held the tone of a parent reproving a daredevil toddler, but the warmth in his eyes dispelled any concern. Those two were going to make one heck of a pair.

The ship's horn tooted and slowly the island-sized craft began to move.

"Shall we watch from upstairs?" Luke extended his hand to Sharla.

"Good idea."

"We'll stay here." Sophia raised her glass. "I wouldn't mind another drink. You two run along and have fun."

He escorted Sharla away from the throngs of passengers leaning over the top deck rail to view the dockside activity and stopped at an isolated spot aft on the big ship. Neither spoke as their floating hotel slowly pulled away, the island of St. Thomas growing smaller with every passing minute. He couldn't decide what to do or say.

Biding his time was something he was very good at.

Timing was everything in the military. A sailor didn't have to have the training of a SEAL to understand that basic concept. But the detailed planning of a mission in enemy territory suddenly seemed to be a cakewalk compared to when and how to address what was on his mind. And heart.

Taking the first step, he moved his hand to cover hers and was delighted to have her immediately thread her fingers with his.

"I've been thinking," tumbled from each of them.

Raw fear caught in his throat. He had to go first. Had to tell her about his plans before she could tell him good-bye. He had to. When she politely smiled and said, "You go first," relief washed over him as quickly as panic had only moments before.

"It doesn't look like George and Gloria are going to be scamming anyone else for a good long while," he said. Not heart-winning prose, but a start.

"Thank heavens for that."

"For years I've focused on the global picture of protecting my country. Never thought a man of my training could do much good here at home."

Sharla's lips tightened, and her grip on his hand lightened, ready to slip away. "I understand."

"No." He squeezed tighter. Unwilling to lose the small connection. "I don't think you do. I had fun. Except for the part where I thought I could lose you forever. Herbie and I enjoyed every step of taking down those snakes. It's a real adrenaline kick knowing some other group of senior citizens won't lose their life savings to George and Gloria down the road."

Head slightly tipped to one side, deep creases formed between her brows, Sharla studied him like a scientist analyzing long-awaited test results.

Results that made no sense to her. Or perhaps results she didn't like. The latter heightened the nerves already tangling in his gut. "I think I can make a difference. A real difference in people's lives. So does Herbie."

The frown deepened. "I don't understand."

Tugging on their linked hands, he pulled her closer.

Close enough that he could feel the light brush of her breath against his chin, the rise of her chest as she sucked in air, then held it.

"It's time for a change. Time to let the younger guys save the world."

Her deep long-held breath whooshed out, and she blinked. Hope shining in her eyes. "What kind of change?"

"It's time *home* meant more than a mailing address. Someplace close to my brother so he can remember what I look like. And someplace close to you."

Her brows shot up; her mouth fell open, and, if he'd been sure that surprised look was because she was pleased and not one of *oh, no*, he would have laughed.

"I, I don't think… I mean—"

"We haven't had very much time together, and we still have a lot more to learn about each other. But I'd like the chance." A strand of hair blew into her face, and he carefully brushed it away, tucking it behind her ear. "I wanted to break the sleeze in the Panama hat's neck with my own two hands for even daring to touch you. The idea of never having another day with you screwed with my head." *And heart.* "I want to get to know you better. And when I think I know all there is to know, I want to learn more. I'd like a chance at forever."

The feel of Luke's fingers lightly brushing against Sharla's cheek left a trail of tingles down her spine all the way to her toes. Everything in her wanted to scream yes, yes, yes! But some small part of her brain scrambled to interpret everything he'd said. Starting with how he and Herbie could make a real difference.

Luke ran the back of his hand along her jaw. "I can't promise you that I won't get hit by a bus or become some medical statistic, but I *can* promise that you won't have to worry about where I go to work every day. I'll never be wheels up again."

"Wheels up?"

His hand dropped in search of hers. Fingers woven together, his thumb gently swirled across the already hypersensitive underside of her wrist. "*Wheels up* is when a team gets called on a mission. We'd have hours to report for duty and be gone. It's hard on a marriage. Wives don't know where their husbands are going or when they'll be back."

"Or if they'll be back." Her voice came out low and scratchy.

"You work in the ER, right?"

She nodded.

"How many families have you seen torn up at the sudden death of a loved one? Car accident. Heart attack. Whatever."

"Too many."

"Any of them teachers? Accountants? Maybe a plumber?" His gaze bore into her with an intensity she'd only seen once before, when he had come flying through the café door searching for her.

"Probably." She knew where he was going with this. But it was different. Not the same thing… Or was it? She was an ordinary nurse who, only a few hours ago, had almost gotten her head blown off by a crazed crook. "What exactly do you and Herbie have in mind?"

Luke knew he'd made progress when the deep furrow between Sharla's brows gave way to a smooth surface. All he had to do was pitch the last bit and pray for a smile. "For starters Herbie has a friend who just moved to a nursing home. Herbie has some suspicions about the quality of care. There's also a resident who wants to know what her son is doing with all the money he keeps asking her for."

"Seems pretty tame work for a big bad SEAL."

"There's more."

"More?"

"Sophia thinks you need a better security system."

"Me?" The word came out just above a whisper.

He tucked that rogue strand of hair behind her ear again and leaned close enough to hear her breath catch. "She thinks your current alarm system is outdated."

"She does?" Her gaze darted from his eyes to his lips and back.

"She seems to think you need something more

encompassing, newer, stronger.”

"Stronger?”

"A security system that can chase away the bad guys. And the ghosts.” He didn't give her another chance to respond. Pulling her tightly against him, he let his mouth find hers. And, dear Lord, she tasted like heaven and hope. And home.

If they hadn't been in public in broad daylight, he would have continued a path down her neck. Lingered on the pulse point calling his name before moving on to her shoulder. But this isolated spot aboard ship wasn't isolated enough. He could hear the sound of approaching footsteps. A pair. Judging by the casual pace, another couple seeking a little privacy to enjoy the departing view—and each other.

Grudgingly he pulled away, his forehead dropping slowly to hers, his breath ragged, and the blood in his veins still rushing south. "What do you say we finish this conversation some place more private?”

"That depends.”

"On?” He lifted his head to read her expression.

The longing in her dark eyes slid away, giving place to an amused sparkle. "Is this a test run of my new security system?”

"Yes, ma'am. Installation is free. And I come with a lifetime warranty.”

"There's no way around this. I need a bigger suitcase.” Sharla dropped her hands to her hips and shook her head.

From behind her, Luke's arms wound around her waist. "Pack the souvenirs, leave the clothes.” He nuzzled her neck. "You won't need them anyway.”

"Has anyone mentioned you have a one-track mind?”

"Yes, ma'am.” He spun her around and captured her mouth in a breath-stealing kiss.

Pulling away and smacking him lightly on the arm, she held back a smile. "You promised not to distract me if I let you help me pack. Just for your information, that's distracting."

"I certainly hope so."

With a quick peck on the tip of his nose, Sharla turned to stare at the overflowing luggage. "This is just going to have to wait. Nana and Herbie are expecting us to meet them for trivia."

"Oh, I forgot to mention that Sophia said to meet them at Herbie's cabin, and we'd leave from there."

"That's different." Hefting one shoulder in a halfhearted shrug, she shook her head, and followed Luke out the door and upstairs to the tenth floor.

Luke rapped on the door. From the other side Sharla could hear Sophia laughing. The sound of her grandmother's happiness made her smile.

"Oh, good. You made it." Sophia gestured them inside the room and moved next to Herbie. The two were grinning at each other like a couple of besotted teens.

It had been great fun for Sharla to watch her grandmother and Herbie grow even closer this last week. With Gloria and George behind bars, and Luke's assurance that his contacts had frozen not just the accounts Nana had found but several others as well, it all had made the last half of their cruise all the more enjoyable.

And as usual Nana had pegged it. Gloria finally confessed to almost having amassed enough money to abandon George and live the remainder of her life worry-free.

Sharla simply didn't get it. There had to be millions in all those accounts. How much money did any one person really need?

Herbie cleared his throat. He and Nana stood side by side, holding hands, their backs to the window. "Why don't you both have a seat?"

Sharla shot a quick glance at Luke before following Herbie's direction.

"Okay." Nana smiled. "We have news. As you know, after the cruise I'm going to New York."

Sharla nodded.

"Well, Herbie thought it might be fun to come with me to meet Leticia and some of my old friends."

Herbie added, "Instead of flying home, I also suggested we take a nice drive back to Florida. Pass through Philly and my old Georgia stomping grounds. Teach your grandmother to do a little fishing."

Fishing? Nana? But the way the woman smiled up at Herbie, apparently Nana thought that was a peachy idea.

"So if you have no objections," Nana continued, "you'll have the house to yourself for another month or so."

"A month?"

"We're going to take our time driving south," Herbie explained.

It took Sharla a few seconds to process the idea, but it only seemed fair. If Luke was coming to Florida to visit his brother—and her—then Herbie should be able to do the same with Nana in New York. Pushing to her feet, Sharla approached her grandmother and wrapped her arms around her, then moved over to give Herbie a big old bear hug too. "I'm trusting you to keep her out of trouble."

Herbie laughed. "You can count on me."

"There's actually a little more news." Nana sidled closer, leaning into the curve of Herbie's arm. "After we return to Florida, we're getting married."

Okay, *that* Sharla wasn't expecting. She backed up and into Luke, who already had her back. "Don't you think that's rushing things a bit?"

"Honey." Nana shook her head. "We're not getting any younger. At our age there's no point in wasting any time."

Luke reached around Sharla to shake Herbie's hand. "Congratulations."

Herbie beamed.

Nana pulled Luke away from Sharla and into her arms for a hug. "You shouldn't waste much time. She's not getting any younger either."

"Nana!"

"Just saying." Nana held up her hands.

"Which reminds me." Herbie turned to open the closet.

Sophia's brows dipped into a scowl. "What are you doing?"

"Getting out my carry-on. I want to give Luke here that address."

Sophia's expression did a complete 180. The deep frown was replaced with a syrupy smile. "Why don't you do that later, dear."

"No." Herbie dragged the bag out and onto the bed.

"Really, Herbie. That can wait."

"It will just take a minute."

Herbie unzipped the bag and, from the inside pocket, pulled out a handful of papers. He took a page from the top and gave it to Luke, then frowned at the manila envelope in the stack beneath it. "What's this?"

"Trivia starts in a few minutes." Sophia took a step aside. "Why don't you put all that away, and we'll head downstairs."

His frown firmly in place, Herbie briefly glanced up at Sophia before opening the envelope and removing a trifold piece of paper. His eyes widened as he pulled out another, and then another, before looking up. "These are bearer bonds."

"What?" Sharla asked.

"Bearer bonds," Luke repeated. "You don't see many of those anymore. They haven't been issued since the laws changed in the eighties. Because they can be cashed in by anyone and not traced, they used to be especially popular with people wanting to hide or launder money."

"Fifty thousand dollars." Herbie looked to Sophia. "The exact amount stolen from Sid."

Sophia's brows lifted high, her smile never faltering. "Imagine that."

Heading up to the lounge to save a table while Herbie and Nana had a word in private, Sharla stepped into the empty elevator and leaned against the wall. "What am I going to do with that woman?"

"I don't know what to tell you." Luke curled his fingers

into hers. When the door closed, he pulled her closer and, with his finger, lifted her chin to see her eyes. "You okay?"

"With the bonds?" She shook her head. "I don't know."

"Fair enough. And with Sophia and Herbie's plans?"

"You know, I think I am." Despite the bond fiasco, the idea of Nana and Herbie made Sharla smile. She'd never seen Nana happier.

"In that case"—he flashed that slow and powerful grin—"I've got some news too."

The door opened on the lido lounge deck, but rather then turn toward the final trivia game of the day, Luke tugged her to his side and led them out onto the open deck.

A nervous knot twisted in her stomach. "Am I going to like this?"

"I hope so." Leaning against the railing, he lifted her hand into his and kissed her knuckles. "I sent in my resignation. This morning I received confirmation. It's official. I am no longer an employee of the US government."

She'd known this was his and Herbie's new plan, but deep down she feared when they returned to real life that Luke would change his mind and go back to saving the world one terrorist at a time.

He pulled out the paper Herbie had given him. "This is a lead for office space in Weston."

"That's by me."

He bobbed his head. "There's also an apartment for rent on Hacienda Terrace."

"I'm around the corner."

He nodded again. "Or…" His mouth tipped up in that confident half smile. "I could wait for Sophia and Herbie to find their own place, and then rent her room." That one charming brow rose high on his forehead, his eyes twinkling.

She bit back a smile. "Pretty presumptuous, don't you think?"

"You heard what your grandmother said. We're not getting any younger."

"Speak for yourself, buster." Lifting their entwined

hands, she waited for a sense of panic to set in. For fear to rob her breath. Any indication that things were moving too fast, too crazy. Too *something*. But the only thing filling her was an utter and complete sense of calm.

"I'll check out the apartment." Luke's smile held, but she could see the disappointment in his eyes. "Maybe look for something closer to the new office. I know apartments go fast, but I'm sure I can get something not too far."

He continued talking but all she heard was the blood rushing through her veins. Now she could taste fear. Fear of losing Luke. Fear he'd settle into a new way of life, and she wouldn't be a part of it. Fear that not letting him fully into her life could be the biggest mistake she'd ever make. "No."

"Excuse me?" Brows creased in confusion, the man looked absolutely adorable.

"No don't rent that apartment just yet. I think you may be right."

"About?"

"I strongly suspect I'll be needing a new roommate sooner than later."

Luke's face lit up like a kid with a new litter of puppies about one second before he pulled her in close and flashed his I'm-too-cute-to-resist smile. "Yes, ma'am. Lt. Luke Chapman volunteering for roommate duty, ma'am."

His lips came crashing down on hers, and, somewhere in the rising tide of sensations rushing over her, she knew a lifetime of Luke Chapman wouldn't be long enough.

EPILOGUE

(takes place after Aloha Texas)

From the living room of US Navy Chief Billy Everrett's house in Kona, Lt. Brent Callahan had a clear view of the deck, the sandy beach in the distance and Brooklyn slipping his arm around his wife's waist while nuzzling her neck. The scene resembled a travel poster promoting honeymoons in Paradise.

Except of course Billy's home wasn't a honeymoon hotel; yet it was on loan from one friend to another. And tonight the honeymooners opened the doors for a family-style barbecue with both old and new friends.

"Have you ever seen two more adorable people?" Maile Everrett, Billy's mother, could do commercials for *Come to Hawaii*. Always dressed in bright floral garb, she never lacked for a welcoming smile. "It does a mother's heart good to see such love. Gives me hope that even sailing the world with the navy, my son will settle down with a nice girl someday."

"What about nice boys for your daughters?" Brent looked across the deck to where the smiling newlywed couple chatted with the two youngest Everrett sisters.

"I'm not worried about them." Maile laughed loud and hard and turned to his former EOD pal Nick Harper standing beside him. "Though I am waiting to see which one you fall in love with."

"Sorry, ma'am." Nick raised his glass to her. "Against the rules. No fraternization with a buddy's sister."

"I'm not talking fraternization, young man. I'm talking marriage."

Ava, the oldest of the Everrett girls, sidled up and

kissed Nick on the cheek. "Good heavens, Mom. Which one of us are you trying to marry off now?"

"Me." Nick shoved his thumb into his chest. "You're off the hook. For now."

Much like her mother, Ava had a deep-in-her-throat laugh that could lift even the heaviest of hearts and could make a man rethink the rules about a buddy's sister. But love and marriage were not in the cards for men like Brent. He'd come close once and learned no woman liked her man to have a mistress, even if it was the US Navy.

"You behaving yourself, sailors?"

"Always," both men echoed.

"Liars." Still grinning, Ava smacked Nick lightly on the arm, the same way she would her brother Billy. "So how come you're in town for this little soiree without my big brother?"

A valid question since King Kona's sisters all probably knew that normally, when one member of an EOD team was on leave, they all were.

"Luck of the draw," Nick answered.

And a valid response, since Brent knew half of Nick's team, including Billy, was currently attached to another SEAL unit for an as-yet-undetermined amount of time. Information neither he nor Nick was at liberty to share. Information not even he would have known had it not almost been his SEAL time they'd been assigned to. Instead, Nick and the rest of his team were doing a special security detail at Pearl. A short hop to Kona. For Brent the timing to attend this soiree with a few of his team mates had simply been right.

"I'd like to take this opportunity to point out," Maile waved her finger between Brent and Ava, "you two make a lovely couple." Billy's mom flashed a cheeky grin and ran the back of her hand gently down her daughter's arm. Across the way Luke dipped his wife in a dramatic kiss before lovingly patting her bottom and lingering to watch her head inside the house. "And on that note, I'm going to see if the bride needs help in the kitchen."

Keeping an eye on her mother as she waddled away,

Ava shook her head, but the smile never faltered. "Sorry about that. I swear Mom has marriage and grandchildren on the brain."

"No big deal." Brent made light of Maile's observation. "That's what mothers do."

"Yours too?"

He nodded. "I'm one of five children. All single. Mom can play matchmaker in two different languages. Never a pretty sight."

Ava gave up another of those deep in the belly laughs and turned to Nick. "You too?"

His buddy shook his head. "Not really. I think she's cutting me some slack because I'm busy saving the world."

Ava rolled her eyes heavenward and took a sip of her mimosa.

"Seriously," nick continued, "I think she recognizes her chances are higher with my sister, so Madeleine gets the brunt of Mom's quest for grandbabies."

"Glad you could make it, man. It's been too long." Brooklyn slapped Nick on the back then glanced at Ava. "Am I interrupting something?"

Shaking his head, Nick gestured at Ava. "Billy's sister Ava. This is the recently ball-and-chained groom, Luke Chapman."

"How do you do?" Ava ignored Nick's ball-and-chain remark. She had an easy way about her, Brent liked that. Again, too bad he wasn't the marrying kind.

"Nice to meet you and, for the record"—Brooklyn turned to Nick—"very happily chained. I'm telling you, man, find the right woman and it makes all the difference in the world."

"Oh, dear," Ava raised a finger to her lips, "please don't let my mother hear you. She'll have us all paired off like Noah's ark within the hour. As a matter of fact, I think I'll go find her and make sure she stays far, far away from all this happily ever after *girl* talk."

"Girl, huh." Nick smacked her backside as she walked away.

Surprised by the playfulness between the two, Brent

turned to Nick. "You friendly with Billy's sister?"

Nick almost choked on his own spit. "Do I look like I want my privates cut off?"

Brooklyn howled.

"What was I thinking?" Brent swallowed a laugh. Turning to the groom, he lifted his chin toward the house. "Glad I could be here. Sharla seems really nice. Congratulations."

"Thanks. Took me two months too long to convince her that I was marriage material, but, with a little help from her grandmother, Sharla finally let me catch her."

Now that was a sight Brent would have liked to have seen. "So, what now? Still with The Company?"

"Negative. I don't want Sharla to get a call one day that I'm not coming home, and all she has to show for it is a star on a wall."

Brent could relate. Too many SEAL wives had been told their husbands died on a training mission when the truth was far from it. "Reactivating with Uncle Sam?"

He shook his head. "No. Her grandmother's husband is a retired cop. We work pretty well together. We've got an interesting combo of contacts, if you know what I mean."

Smothering a smile, Brent didn't even want to begin to consider the sort of contacts a former SEAL-turned-spook and an ex-cop might have.

Brooklyn's gaze drifted to his wife carrying a platter of fruit from the kitchen, and both Brent and Nick waited patiently for their smiling friend to finally drag his attention back to the conversation.

"It strikes me that," Brooklyn reached in his pocket, "while you guys are saving the world from annihilation, someone here needs to help clean up the trash."

"Cop?" Brent asked.

"PI." Brooklyn handed Nick a card. Brooklyn Security.

Brent looked up at Brooklyn, once again watching his new wife, and asked, "You're okay with this?"

"Very."

Brent stared down at the card. A whole new life for a woman. And the guy seemed happy about it. Really happy.

Brent slipped the business card into his breast pocket and, looking over Brooklyn's shoulder at the killer view of the Kona shore, considered for the first time in a long time that maybe a new life outside the navy wasn't such a bad idea.

Not a bad idea at all.

EXCERPT FROM

FLIRTING WITH PARADISE

"Would you two get a room?" Brad Peyton couldn't even hit the John without his high school buddy Forrest John Maplewood making a move on the girl. Some things never changed. Well, except one. This girl was John's wife.

In the hallway of the tastefully refurbished Hawaiian home, Ava sprang away from her husband. Much like a teen caught making out on Lovers' Lane by a cop with a flashlight, she patted her hair and smoothed her dress, a delightful rush of pink filling her cheeks. Brad could definitely see why John grinned like an unrepentant fool. They had a good thing going.

"Billy and Angela should be here any minute. I'd better check on that lasagna." Ava slid out of her husband's grip and hurried to the kitchen.

Brad only allowed his gaze to trail Ava as long as was socially acceptable to stare at his good friend's wife. It wasn't that he had a thing for her or anything; he just wondered vaguely if there would ever be a woman in his life who made him feel the way John Maplewood looked.

Not that it mattered. At almost thirty-five years old, Brad wasn't ready to settle down. But watching John Maplewood, the master of charming and aloof, totally enraptured by one woman, made Brad question if it was time for him to reconsider. Ever since the festive wedding celebrations, with every visit to Kona, Brad expected to see their blissful union deteriorating. So far, the only conclusion he'd made was that, if he could package whatever these two had and sell it, he'd be richer than the British royal family. And happy as hell.

"Wunkel John!" From the back hall a squealing toddler came hurrying as fast as she could waddle without breaking into a trot—a cat hung precariously in her grip. The poor animal's toes barely touched the floor, scurrying like a hamster on a wheel to keep from being dragged by the cutest little girl with enormous brown eyes.

Brad found himself squatting to the child's level, a small part of him hoping she'd come share with him, even if he hadn't a clue what to do with her.

"Sorry about that." A long-haired brunette came hurrying after the little spitfire. "She spotted the cat the second we were in the kitchen door and before I could take a breath she'd nabbed Peaches and was off."

Grinning, John hunched down in front of his niece. "You like Peaches, don't you?"

The sweet-faced child bobbed her head, squeezing the furry feline more tightly. John's eyes momentarily flared with the same concern Brad had felt that the animal might lash out. When the cat merely glanced up, somewhat forlorn, John blew out a steady breath of air and gently eased her hold on the animal.

"We've tried to explain that Peaches is not a doll," Angela shook her head, and leaned over her little girl. "If you insist on carrying Peaches, you need to hold all of her in your arms."

Gently *Wunkle John* freed the feline from the little girl's near-strangling grasp and curled her into the child's arms. "See, like this."

The friendlier stance lasted all of a few seconds before a squirming cat found herself once again in a choke hold with her toes barely touching ground.

Billy looked pleadingly at his wife. Brad wasn't sure but from the doe-eyed look on the man's face, he suspected he didn't want to be the one to take the cat away from his little girl. The former Navy EOD tech could dismantle bombs but didn't want to tangle with a toddler. That a tiny little thing had a bruiser like Billy wrapped so easily around her finger teased a smile from Brad's lips.

"Time to let go, Sweetie." Angela slid the kitty away from her daughter and with a single stroke along its back—no doubt in appreciation for not scratching the hell out of her daughter—the freed kitty darted away just as Billy whirled the laughing toddler into his arms.

The next thing Brad knew, John had zoomed in, and, passing the girl back and forth between them, the two men seemed to be playing an animated version of here comes the plane. The spray of giggles that followed siphoned every last drop of stress from Brad's body and had him grinning like the fool on the hill. That pang of doubt that had tapped in Brad's gut a moment ago thumped a little harder now. Maybe he *was* missing out.

"And this"—winning final custody of the little girl, Billy blew raspberries onto the swath of his daughter's exposed tummy—"is why I take advantage of every moment alone with my wife."

"Sounds like you're bucking for number two," John teased.

"Not a bad idea." Billy winked at his own wife who flushed several shades of rose.

Isabella scrambled from her dad's arms and, this time in a full trot, called happily after Peaches.

The picture looked pretty. But the reality, for most people, was more akin to the real housewives of some depraved city. Screaming spouses, spoiled children, and pets that peed on the expensive leather furniture. John had married into an amazing family. His newfound Kona clan were a happy anomaly, unlikely to be repeated. And certainly not by Brad. No, he reminded himself. City lights, high-stake deals, and no-strings-attached women made up his happy world. Suburban domesticity was not for him. Nieces, nephews, or otherwise.

"Just a few more minutes and we can sit down to dinner." Ava came back into the front room that doubled as a waiting area for her architectural offices and living room during non business hours. They had a small apartment upstairs, but Brad had learned on one of his earlier visits that when entertaining more than two, they took full advantage of the sprawl of the first floor.

"Need help with anything?" John snatched his wife's hand and squeezed.

At first this humble domestic side of John had taken a little getting used to for Brad. John, like Brad, had been raised in a full-on mansion with servants and every opportunity for some serious spoiling. All grown up, the man had lived in LA in a two story penthouse in a building John owned, and from what Brad remembered, he'd never seen the guy open the fridge door, never mind help with a dinner party. Somehow, John had slid easily into this cozy world of domestic middle class bliss. Brad wasn't sure why it worked so well, but he had to admit, it was one of the most welcoming homes he'd had the pleasure of visiting.

A flash of bright green and yellow frill darted past Brad from across the hall with little Isabella squealing gleefully in the wake of the cat now sporting a doll's dress.

Ava blew out an amused sigh. "Who knew when that scrawny stray adopted us she'd prove to be the most patient animal in the world."

"Apparently," The little girl's mother shook her head. "Izzy has clearly discovered the joy of motherhood. That poor cat has been dressed up, wrapped up, bottle-fed, burped…"

"Burped?" Brad asked.

"*Very* patient." John smiled.

"Yes," Ava confirmed. "Very."

John's hand fell casually on his wife's arm, but he continued to face Brad. "Didn't expect to see you in Kona so soon after your last visit. Problems with the Royal Palms?"

"As a matter of fact, it's doing so well that I just closed on another beachfront property." All it had taken for Brad to fall in love with the relaxing Hawaiian lifestyle was a single visit to Kona for John and Ava's wedding. When an opportunity to buy into a floundering hotel on the shores of

Paradise landed at his feet, Brad didn't hesitate to buy the Royal Palms.

"I see." John smiled.

"Besides, I needed to work on my tan." Brad flashed his practiced boyish grin. Experience told him it still carried an impact, even if he was far from a boy. The truth was, most of the time one of the acquisitions team would do a final walk-through to evaluate staffing before implementing changes, but this was Paradise.

Ava chuckled. By now she knew him almost as well as her husband did, and, like John, Brad was a no-nonsense businessman who hadn't worked on a tan since spring break during his college years. Truth was, he needed a breather, and Ava probably knew it.

"You can't blame the guy for not sending a grunt." Billy came in from the kitchen with a beer in one hand and an ice filled glass of water for his wife.

"Thanks, dear." Angela took the glass and shared a quick peck on the lips with the former sailor. Maybe there was something in the water on this island. Brad made a mental note to stick with beer or fruit juice on this visit.

"Whatever the reason," Ava tipped her glass of wine at him, "it's always nice to see you."

"Thanks." Spinning a coaster in his hand, he turned to face his longtime friend. "You'll get a kick out of this. Got a call yesterday from one of those reality TV shows."

"As the bachelor or will you be fawning over the bachelorette?" Except for the one hand casually rubbing the inside of his wife's palm, John remained stiff and unmoving.

"Ha, ha. Neither."

"Well it can't be Big Brother," Billy laughed.

John's eyes widened a little. "Don't tell me you're crazy enough to run around the world with a backpack or live in the jungle with only a loin cloth?"

Sputtering with reigned in amusement at his friend's assumptions, Brad set down the coaster and hefted his ankle over his knee. "The show where the head of a company goes incognito to work."

"Oh"—Angela rubbed her hands together—"I love that show. Especially the episodes when the boss makes sweeping changes that affect the whole company. Which of your companies will you infiltrate?"

"None. Apparently the former owner of Paradise Shores Hotel had agreed to participate. I have no such inclination."

"What do you mean, *no*?" Ava's brow crinkled in confusion.

"Don't look so surprised. Why the heck would I want to wear a cheap wig, thick glasses and a fake nose? I already know everything I need to. Once we replace the existing personnel with my people and fully implement my resort standards, it won't take long to turn the outdated and glorified roadside inn into a five-star destination. This walk-through is just a technicality."

"Technicality?" The tone of Ava's voice shifted to one she might use when dealing with an unusually dense underling. "The employees are people with families and bills to pay. They're more than numbers on a spreadsheet. It would do you good to see that for yourself. Besides, some of the TV show participants only need a new hairdo and—"

"Off-the-rack clothes." Brad laughed at the idea. "Like I said, no thanks. I'm not putting on a dog-and-pony show for anyone."

"You'd look good with a new nose," John deadpanned.

"Let me know when *you* go undercover, and then maybe I'll think about it." If Ava and Angela had not been in the room, Brad would have offered a different comeback. Something hitting a little further below the belt.

"I already have. Sort of." John shrugged. "Remember I spent my vacation here in Kona as regular Forrest Maplewood, not CEO John Maplewood. Besides if that doesn't count, Father had all of us work at least one summer in high school for his company. To appreciate the value of a buck. In his infinite wisdom, Ironman Maplewood decided I needed to work with the janitor."

Billy tipped his beer bottle at him. "That explains why you wield a mean mop."

"Ha ha," John teased back.

Angela shrugged at Brad "You have to admit. John's got a point about his visit here. None of us had a clue he wasn't just an ordinary construction guy."

"I think you should do it." Ava stared at Brad. "It will be good for you and the hotel."

He could hear the dare in her tone, see it in her stare. Blast, she might not be a business mogul, but she had that don't-mess-with-me stare down pat.

"Why would I want to carve out a week or more of my already overloaded schedule? This place is no different than any other hotel we've bought out. We have a proven takeover strategy. I don't have to see the place to know what has to be done."

"It's one thing to be presented with a shiny new toy. It's another thing to be the person who shines it." Ava crossed her arms, and Brad ignored the prideful smile John bestowed on his wife.

"No," Brad repeated more sternly. The whole idea was absurd. By the time he had turned thirty, he'd bought and sold more companies than his old man had in his entire life. Brad didn't need to play doorman to evaluate the latest acquisition.

"She's right." John Maplewood was an imposing man who could get his way with just a look.

A look that didn't work on Brad. He shook his head.

A buzzer sounded from the kitchen, and Ava pushed to her feet. "Dinner will be served in ten."

"I'll go get Izzy." Angela stood and smiled at her sister-in-law. "The cat will be thrilled."

Crossing the room, Ava paused at Brad's side. "Every good CEO should know what it's like to be at the bottom of the totem pole." Then she walked away.

Shifting his gaze from his wife's departing back to his brother-in-law who merely shrugged and smiled, and finally settling on Brad, like the cocky jock he'd always been back in school, John cast a wry grin in his friend's direction. "Afraid you can't cut it?"

"That look doesn't work on me anymore."

John's grin grew. He leaned back into the leather love

seat. "I dare you. No TV cameras. No gimmicks. Just you, a false name, and two weeks punching a clock."

This was ridiculous. Why was he even discussing something so absurd? All through high school, he and John had one-upped each other with dares and challenges. Stupid inconsequential things at first, like who could eat more hotdogs without barfing, but, by senior year, they'd coaxed each other into almost everything regardless of cost or risk, but that was years ago. They'd both moved on to the real world. Matured. But still, the look in John's gaze sent Brad spiraling back to their days in the hallowed halls of one of the East Coast's most elite prep school, where pissing contests seemed to be the favored pastime. There was no reason for Brad to do this. None. He had nothing to prove. To anyone.

John's smile slipped, his expression blank, his thoughts unreadable, as he leaned forward, pinning Brad with his gaze. "Unless of course, you don't think you're man enough?"

Billy burst out laughing, just as his wife and daughter walked into the room. "Oh to be a fly on the wall for this one."

Brad wasn't going to do it. There was no reason. No reason at all. Except maybe the two men glaring at him.

MEET CHRIS

Author of dozens of contemporary novels, including the award winning Aloha Series, Chris Keniston lives in suburban Dallas with her husband, two human children, and two canine children. Though she loves her puppies equally, she admits being especially attached to her German Shepherd rescue. After all, even dogs deserve a happily ever after.

More on Chris and her books can be found at www.chriskeniston.com.

Follow Chris on facebook at ChrisKenistonAuthor or on twitter @ckenistonauthor.

Join Chris' newsletter! Enjoy inside peeks and photographs from Chris' world and stories. Some times she'll thank her subscribers with a free copy of a new 99 cent flirt.

Please, if you enjoyed reading Shell Game, consider helping other readers find the Aloha Romance series by taking a moment to leave a review. Reviews are a blessing to authors and readers alike. Even just a few words will do! Thank you.